Y0-CCW-104

New Hanover
County Public
Library

The Man
with
My Cat

The Man
with
My Cat

Paul Engleman

ST. MARTIN'S MINOTAUR
NEW YORK

This is a work of fiction. Any inference of similarity to actual living people is attributable to wishful thinking or paranoia on the part of the reader.

Design by Nancy Resnick

ISBN 0-312-24651-X

First Edition: January 2000

10 9 8 7 6 5 4 3 2 1

For Joe and Lou
(be sure to share)

Acknowledgments

Many thanks to the men behind Phil Moony—Ed Reardon and Marc Levison—and the man behind Phull Moony— Mark Engleman; and to folks who have helped in many ways: Barb Carney, Helen Frangoulis, Tony Judge, Keith Kahla, Lucy Lemmer, Pat McGuire, Mike Murphy, Chris Napolitano, Barbara Nellis, Steve Randall, John Rezek, Chuck Savage, Jim Trupin, Susan B. Walton.

The Man
with
My Cat

One

I drive down Clark Street at a crawl, gazing at the entrance to the Anti-Cruelty Society building as we pass. This is my third time circling the block. I'm not looking for a parking space. I'm trying to find my nerve.

I glance at the cat carrier in the backseat and catch a glimpse of Phull behind the caged door. He lets out a pathetic whine. That doesn't help me any.

Phull is my cat. My father's cat, actually. But Dad died last year and left me two of his most treasured possessions: his car and his cat. We're driving in his car now. It's a Chrysler LeBaron.

Phull is a Maine coon. I'm told he's a much better model than a LeBaron, but I don't know much about cats or cars. I do know that the LeBaron doesn't leak.

I've played this scene out once before, right down to the detail of parking at a hydrant and heading for the shabby little tavern with the Old Style sign to think things over.

There are two details different from the last time I set out to put Phull away. One, my backup vet appointment—just in case I lose my nerve—is with a new vet. Two, just to make sure I don't lose my nerve, Frankie's with me.

Frankie's my wife. She hates cats. Well, actually, her eyes, nose and throat hate cats. Her heart goes out to them. But during allergy season, Frankie's eyes, nose and throat are much bigger than her heart.

There's a long story behind why my father called the cat Phull. For now, I'll just tell you that my name is Phil Moony and Dad thought it would be pretty phunny to have a cat named Phull Moony. After what Phull has put me through since Dad died, Frankie says I should change my name to Phool.

Frankie is quite the witty gal. She has to be, she's a writer. She's also very observant, so I don't even get two steps from the car before she notices that I'm heading in the opposite direction from the Anti-Cruelty building.

"Where are you going, Phil?"

"Maybe we should have a drink and think it over."

One of the things Frankie and I have in common is that we do some of our best thinking over a drink. We also like a drink even when we're not trying to think.

She sighs heavily. "We've already thought it over, Phil."

Before Frankie gets painted as the bad cop here, I should point out that she has come along specifically to play that role. I asked her to do so. The fact is, if Phull hadn't been my father's cat, I wouldn't be thinking twice about sending him off to the great wherever. I've got allergies too. And I've gotten very tired of sinking my socks into the mushy bogs Phull has created on the basement carpet. Frankie is amazed that I dare to go down there without shoes. But every time I consider putting Phull out of my misery, I get to feeling like I'd be killing a part of my father that lives on. Bad karma is what it is.

"You know what Albie used to say," I tell her: "There's always room to think some more."

Albie was Frankie's father. He died a few years ago and left her the house that Phull's been redecorating. He left me with about five thousand aphorisms, recalled in his last days,

2

which he spent mostly with me, drinking Old Grand-dad and playing cards.

Frankie offers me her sarcastic look, an affected smile with a precise measuring of boredom and contempt. When she has that expression, she looks a lot like Albie.

"Albie also used to say, 'There's always time to drink some more.' And he eventually proved to be wrong about that, didn't he?"

"Yeah, but he had a good run at it."

"You go have a drink," she says, grasping the handle of the carrier. "I'll go have Phull taken care of."

"You know I can't let you do that."

We've thought this part through over lots of drinks. If Phull is going to be put away, I have to be the one to do it. It's a matter of principle, and Frankie understands that. She reaches out and takes my hand. "Honey, I'll take care of it. You go have a drink."

I can tell by the softness in her tone that she's trying to spare me the pain. This isn't one of those things that she'll hold over my head. It's a generous, loving offer, no strings attached.

As I glance at the carrier, I can feel principle and chickenshit coming to blows inside me. Just then Phull tries to get in his point of view with a few pitiful meows.

Frankie shoots him a glance and wags her finger. "You stay out of this."

"Yeah, it's only your fate we're discussing," I tell him. Then I hear myself ask her, in my most chickenshit, un-principled voice, "Are you sure you don't mind?"

"Honey, just go," she says.

I turn away and don't look back. If I did, I know I'd start to bawl. I wouldn't be bawling for the cat. I'd be bawling for my father.

The tavern hasn't changed much since the last time I was in it. The four old fellows parked on stools opposite beer cans just might be the same guys who were here six months ago. Two of them are nodding off, the other two are just nodding. One of the guys nodding off is the bartender. He awakens to the clatter of my change dropping on the bar.

I start in soul-searching with the help of Jim Beam. It's the high-end bourbon here at Lou's. (That's the name of the place and the bartender.) Actually, my search isn't going any deeper than the first layer of rationalization. Mr. Beam has provided a lot of solace for me in this area over the years. When I say or do something I probably should regret, Jim's often there to back me up.

If Phull's penchant for peeing anyplace he pleases were his only behavioral shortcoming, I probably wouldn't be going through with it. But Phull's got some other unsavory tendencies.

The one that bothers Frankie the most is his habit of lounging in an old armchair—it was my father's thank God—and licking himself into a frenzy. She says the thing that bugs her about it is his lack of manners. He doesn't care who sees him, even when he's going at top speed, which we've come to call Phull Throttle.

Me, I don't have any problem with Phull's chair antics. The habit of his that I object to is more basic: He sprays.

The first time I took Phull to a vet was to take care of this problem. But at his age, which we figure is about eight, neutering is not recommended. Anesthetizing an older cat involves some risk, and the vet didn't think it was a risk worth taking. Especially after I made the mistake of disclosing Phull's deepest, darkest secret: Despite his powerful physique and manly swagger, the poor guy shoots blanks. He's as sterile as a Band-Aid.

To the vet's way of thinking, there was no need to fix a cat who didn't pose any threat of knocking up the other cats in the neighborhood. I couldn't bring myself to tell her it wasn't the neighborhood cats I was concerned about, it was the walls of my house. Something in her manner suggested that "convenience of owner" was not an acceptable reason for putting Phull under the knife.

I know this sounds sexist, but I think I could have convinced her to go through with it if she had been a man. A male vet could relate to the horror of going to grab a screwdriver and finding out your whole toolroom's been spritzed. My power drill hasn't worked right since the day that happened.

So Vet Number One talked me out of it. She also talked me out of twenty-five bucks. But I'm sure she thought she was saving me money. Fixing Phull would have cost a hundred.

I'm finishing off my second drink when Frankie arrives.

"So how did it go?" I try my best to sound casual, but I can feel my voice cracking.

She doesn't reply, but her drink order provides all the answer I need. She asks the bartender for a glass of cheap red wine. When Frankie's in her cheap red wine mood, it means things haven't been going too well.

Lou says that's the only kind of wine they've got. As proof he holds up a half-gallon jug. "They've got red zinfandel now, did you know that?" he asks.

It takes us a moment to realize he's kidding. When he sees that we get it, he refills my glass and says it's on him.

I wait until Frankie downs half her wine before I probe for information. "Spare me the details, but do tell me what happened."

"He's out in the car," she says, nodding to where the window to the street would be if the bar had any windows.

"What?"

"You heard me. He's out in the damn car."

Right now, this seems like the best of all possible outcomes for me. Not only is my father's cat not dead, but I have good fresh ammunition to use on Frankie.

"You lost your nerve," I say.

"No, I didn't. The place was crowded. I wasn't in the mood to wait on line."

"Admit it: You lost your nerve."

"Hey, don't gloat."

"Am I gloating? Sorry."

"Of course you're gloating." She shrugs. "I left the car unlocked. I figured someone might steal him."

"With our luck, someone will just steal his box."

"Try being optimistic for a change. Maybe we'll get real lucky and someone will steal the car." Frankie's been itching to buy an import.

Two

It didn't come as any surprise to me when Phull started sprinkling the basement as if it were the front lawn. My father sometimes referred to him as P. H., which stood for Pee Here. He also called him P. T.—Pee There. But I didn't realize how bad the problem was until I cleared out Dad's effects after he passed away.

At that time I saw it as kind of a blessing. My father had accumulated a ton of papers and magazines, and Phull's leaky legacy made the sorting process move along a whole lot faster.

Phull is not his original name, by the way. My father wasn't his original owner. He took Phull in as a favor to Rochelle, a neighbor lady who became his close friend after my mother died.

The relationship started out with Rochelle stopping by now and then with something for him to eat, and it soon escalated to daily dining. Rochelle was a good cook and my father was a good eater. My father mixed a good drink, and Rochelle liked nothing better than mixing good drinking and cooking. With his mixing and eating and her cooking and drinking, they had a nice little arrangement going for a while there.

During Rochelle's tenure the cat had been named Edwin—after her dead husband. My father said he changed it because Edwin was a dumb name for a cat. But I also knew that he never liked the original Edwin. When I was growing up, Dad couldn't mention Edwin's name without adding that he was a shitheel, and Edwin eventually came to be known around our house simply as the Shitheel.

This had a lot to do with Edwin once getting out of line with my mother at the Fourth of July block party. My father had a few pops too many, and when Edwin got fresh, Dad decided to pop him a few times. My mother was embarrassed, but they later came to refer to it as the year Dad provided the fireworks.

From what my father told me late in his life, Rochelle also regarded Edwin as something of a shitheel. Her attraction for my father apparently began about two seconds after he started in thumping him. Edwin was killed by a train about ten years ago. He tried to jump the gate to catch the seven-fifteen but he slipped and the train caught him instead. About two days after the funeral, Rochelle began breeding cats. Probably out of guilt, she named one of her studs Edwin.

As luck would have it, Edwin the cat shared something in common with Edwin the Shitheel. Rochelle confided to Dad that the reason they never started a family was because of "Edwin's problem." Rochelle's prize stud turned out to be as big a dud as her husband. That's another reason why my father thought it would be funny to call him Phull—he was an empty vessel. Dad's sense of irony and contempt for Edwin lasted to the end.

Dad and Rochelle's little arrangement reached its end about two years ago. Rochelle had a terrible fall and ended up doing the tragic two-step—first the hospital, then the nursing home. Rochelle felt guilty about the idea of putting

8

Edwin away. So she asked my father to take care of him—just temporarily.

The last thing in the world my father wanted at that stage of his life was a cat. But he would have felt guilty saying no. I think the fact that Rochelle had fallen on her way home from Happy Hour at his place added to his guilt. By that point in time, Happy Hour was getting underway about ten in the morning.

Needless to say, Rochelle never got out of the nursing home. She barely made it out of the hospital. Once the doctors got a look at her liver, falling and breaking her hip was determined to be the least of her problems. All of her problems came to an end pretty soon after they started performing surgeries on her. About four months after her fall, she landed beside Edwin up at Bohemian National.

With no skill for cooking or drinking, Phull was no substitute for Rochelle. But my father enjoyed his company during the short time he had left. He worried aloud what would happen to the furry little faucet after he died. I had little choice but to promise I'd take him in. After all the crap from me that Dad had to put up with over the years, I was glad to do it.

It's hard to believe one little creature could cause so much guilt in so many people. It's been passed on from Rochelle to my father to me. Now, as I gaze at my wife, I can see that it's moved right along to her. And it all came about because Edwin the Shitheel couldn't wait fifteen minutes for the next goddamn train.

"So," I ask Frankie, "what do you want to do?"

"Don't look at me like that."

"Like what?"

She ignores the question and flags Lou for a refill. The protocol here is that I'm supposed to wait for her to have a sip and her say before I open my mouth.

"Are you positive this new vet isn't just as big a wacko as the last one?" she asks.

9

On my first aborted mission to Anti-Cruelty, I took Phull to a second vet, Dr. Howard. His front door was weighted down with signs saying he accepted Visa, MasterCard and Discover, so I realized I was in trouble right away. He declared Phull in tip-top shape, then used the *S*-word in diagnosing his bladder problem.

That's right: stress.

Doc Howie wasn't at all amused when I said Phull led the least stressful existence of anyone I had ever known. He recommended—I kid you not—taking Phull to a pet counselor. When I reported this to Frankie, she said she thought Phull would be much better off if we just got him a lawyer. Doc Howie, by the way, happened to have a friend in the pet-therapy racket. Then he charged me forty bucks. I put it on my Discover, then canceled the card. By now, I'm in for something like eighty-seven bucks.

I assure Frankie that Vet Number Three is not a wacko. "This is where Pat takes his cats. He says the place is great."

Pat is our friend Pat Ryan. He's a retired cop, a very high-ranking one. I knew Pat first when I worked for the fire department, but Frankie got to know him better when she was a reporter at the *Sun-Times*. Pat was her source for a major exposé on police corruption. Pat took a lot of risks for her—and it caused him plenty of inner turmoil. Although he admired her cause, he didn't see much honor in blowing the whistle. He thought there was a very fine line between whistle-blower and snitch.

Pat was a seminarian before he was a cop, and Frankie regards him almost as a modern-day saint. I guess I do too, though he once double-crossed me.

Pat has four cats, all strays. He calls them Eany, Meany, Miney and Mo. When he heard we were thinking about putting Phull to sleep, he actually offered to take him off our hands. But Frankie wouldn't permit it. She feels it would be a terrible imposition, and she's concerned that Pat is already surrounded by too many of the things. Frankie's still holding out hope that the right girl will come Pat's way, but she's concerned that the cat-infested state of his apartment is a big barrier. Adding our little sprinkler into the mix would douse any spark of hope.

"If Pat says the guy's okay, we can give it one last shot," Frankie says. "But this time we make it clear what we want: We leave him there a couple of days and get all his plumbing totally checked out. And"—she points at me with the index finger on her right hand, the finger that has a sharper nail than the other nine—"we get the little pisser fixed."

She turns on her stool and goes for her wine. "This time no wishy-washy save-the-animals consciousness-raising about the perils of anesthesia. If he comes out of it, he comes home. If he doesn't, it's *buona notte, dolci sogni.* Agreed?"

I smile and nod and nod and nod. I never disagree with Frankie when she speaks Italian.

Three

The vet's name is Dr. Nelson, and his office is located on Lawrence Avenue in one of those generic strip malls with pastel awnings that have become standard in all neighborhood development schemes.

I won't tell you the name of the place, because you'll think I'm crazy for going there.

Oh, I might as well, just so I can relay the alternative name that Frankie comes up with. The place is called the Purr & Bark Veterinary Hospital and Kennel. She wonders if they thought about calling it Scratch & Sniff.

The mall is shaped like an L, with one full leg taken up by Scratch & Sniff and the other sliced into thirds for a White Hen Pantry convenience store, a Mail Boxes, Etc. knockoff and a TCBY that went belly-up and now has a "space available" sign in the window. No particular reason I say this except for the property divvy, but I've got a hunch that Dr. Nelson branched out into real estate in the eighties and owns the whole spread. Until recently—maybe five years ago—it was an undeveloped parcel of land, the kind you used to see all over the far Northwest Side before Orchard Field became

O'Hare and noise abatement became something else for residents to make noise about.

As with most burb-style strips that have sprouted in the city, the parking lot is short about twenty spaces. Rather than compete with the three cars squatting for the next available spot, I opt for curbside illegal at the bus stop. With a Meter Moron prowling the next block, Frankie says I should stay behind the wheel while she goes inside. Since Mayor Dickie privatized the parking collections system, fixing a ticket has become a major pain—more guys to pay off and they're harder to find. Besides that, Frankie's afraid I might turn pussy about putting the fix order in on Phull.

This isn't a neighborhood where I'd expect to see anyone I know. There are no decent restaurants, the bars are strictly functional, and the shops mostly carry mundane merchandise that you can get in any other shopping district in the city. But I can't seem to go anywhere in this town without spotting, or being spotted by, someone I know. Sure enough, as I glance into the passenger-side mirror to get an update on the position of the parking vulture, I see a familiar figure sashaying down the sidewalk in my direction.

If the truth be told, this is someone I don't want to see me, but I'm having trouble taking my eyes off her. It's a problem any hetero guy approaching middle-aged lechery would have. I'm showing considerable restraint by limiting my gaze to the mirror instead of turning my head.

Kadie Thurmond is a champion head-turner, always has been, always will be. Her black hair is about shoulder-length now, a few inches longer than the last time I saw her, two years ago, maybe three. It's blowing across her face in the stiff October breeze, hiding the perfect cheekbones and pale green eyes that I can picture perfectly even if I can't see them.

Kadie is a delightful eyeful all right, but if we make eye contact, I know I'll get an earful. She can chatter like a parakeet and she's cursed with a nervous giggle that can drive a reasonable guy nuts. I speak with authority here, even if some people might not find me so reasonable. I lived with Kadie for about two years, about ten years ago.

That was in the eighties, during the days of cocaine, or at least my days of cocaine. Far as I know, they're still going on for lots of people. In my case, there were very few actual days, but they were spread over a period of about six months. That was about the same length of time I knew Kadie before we moved in together.

Those were mad times. People from all different circles were crossing paths and they were all in search of the same thing: overpriced white powder that screws up your sinuses, taxes your heart and makes everything seem wonderful in thirty-minute bursts. Frankie went through a phase right around the time I did. But we never met. The circles were big and there were lots of them.

I consider myself fortunate that cocaine and I didn't agree. For one thing, my sinuses couldn't take it. For another, the thrill that most people got from it—staying up all night—was something I had to do for my job. (By the way, I never did coke on the job, didn't even think about it.) I did enjoy the idea that people were getting to see the city the way I got to see it twice each week. But the times I did coke, I always ended up wondering how the hell I came to be staying up all night with the jerks I was with. And it was the coke, of course.

They were Kadie's friends mostly, but there were always some stragglers no one could account for or wanted to account for. Typically, it would start in a bar, usually, on a Friday night, with someone saying he knew someone who knew someone who could get some blow. Hours of phone calls later, you'd end up sitting around someone's coffee table with a group of people. As soon as everyone had a couple of lines, they all seemed smart and clever and interesting, no matter how boring they might have seemed earlier in the evening. The feeling would last about twenty minutes, until the coke started to wear off, then everyone would start getting edgy. Suddenly, no one seemed the slightest bit interesting, not even the people you found interesting to start with. The bores, they became even duller than you could have imagined.

Everyone would be watching the guy with the blow, usually your host, the owner of the coffee table. He was often the most boring guy in the group, and your feelings about him would fluctuate wildly—in direct proportion to how often and how generously he was laying out lines. I tended to feel sorry for the host, because each time the coke wore off, I knew he was wondering when the hell these boring people were going to leave. The only way they would leave was if he stopped pouring out coke. As his supply dwindled he'd also be wondering which jerk was going to sneak out without leaving any money. At least that's how I felt on the two occasions Kadie and I ended up hosting a blow party at our apartment.

Kadie's blow period lasted much longer than mine. It was still going on when I moved out. I'm the one that moved, but she sent me packing. Kadie complained that I was no fun as soon as we started living together.

"Of course I'm not," I used to tell her. "I'm not doing any coke."

Watching in the mirror, I can see that Kadie's wearing tight blue jeans, a black leather jacket and what at first looks like a giant necklace. As she moves closer, the necklace begins to look like a giant snake. Kadie did not own a snake when I knew her, but I recall that a college friend of hers did and she was very interested in the snake the night he brought it to our apartment. I'm wondering if she's bringing it to Scratch & Sniff for a checkup.

Objects in the side mirror, as you probably know, appear farther away than they really are. The closer Kadie gets, the more sure I am that I don't want her to see me. It would be much nicer just to see her, to take one long look and one deep breath and wonder for a moment what might have been, then sigh and rejoice that I hooked up with Frankie. But instead of slumping down or looking the other way, I keep angling closer to the passenger side to maintain my full mirrored view. By now I've almost had my visual fill of Kadie, but I'm damn curious about the snake. The idea of Kadie writhing with a snake on her water bed—at least she used to have a water bed—touches a pleasant nerve in me.

The identity of the snake becomes clear at the moment Kadie catches sight of me. Her mirror image suddenly gets so large that I turn to the window for a look, and she's standing right there, staring at me.

"Phil, what are you doing up here?" she asks as I roll down the window.

"I could ask you the same question."

"I had to get a new hose for my vaccuum cleaner." She fingers the hollow plastic head of the snake and points to a store at the end of the block.

Thus ends my Kadie-snake fantasy. For some people, I suppose, the discovery of the vaccuum hose could enhance the fantasy. But not for me, not with Kadie. She was obsessive about dirt. As much time as she spent doing blow, she spent twice as much sucking up dirt.

"I'm waiting for Frankie—my wife," I say. I'm not sure Kadie even knows I got married. "She's dropping off our cat at the vet's."

"You have a cat?" Kadie punctuates the question with her trademark giggle, but it goes on longer than I remember.

I nod. "What's so funny about that?"

"Are you kidding? Don't you remember what happened when you watched Ellyn's cat that time?"

Ellyn Miller was a close friend of Kadie's. They were in nursing school together and both worked at Michael Reese. That's how I met Kadie. She worked in the ER when I was a paramedic on the fire department.

"Oh yeah, that's right," I say. Until Kadie's reminder, I

had managed to suppress the memory of Ellyn's cat.

Kadie giggles hard. "You really had the magic touch, Phil. Agree to watch someone's cat for three days and it's dead in twenty-four hours."

Ellyn's cat, Felix, died while Ellyn and Kadie were away at their nursing school reunion. I didn't want to watch Felix, but Ellyn hated the idea of leaving him in a kennel and Kadie volunteered my services. The vet's diagnosis was distemper, but Ellyn suspected Felix had eaten aspirin that I had carelessly left on the floor of our apartment. Ellyn was a neatnik too.

"Ellyn was so mad at you for that. Do you remember?"

I force a smile. "Yeah, I remember." I don't need to remind Kadie that I was also mad at Ellyn. When I moved out of our apartment, Ellyn moved in. She and Kadie were supposedly just roommates, but it soon became clear that they were a lot closer than that.

Ellyn had a nose problem, and she had a boyfriend named Ace with a serious nose problem. When Ace ran out of coke, he used to get very depressed. The only thing that would bring him out it was to slap Ellyn around. That was right around the time Kadie and I were breaking up. Kadie was spending a lot of time consoling Ellyn, and they came to a mutual decision that they'd be better off without men in their lives.

Believe it or not, I wasn't all that crushed by the idea of being dumped for another woman. Some guys see it as the ultimate rejection—you're so pathetic, you've turned her off to all men. But I found it a refreshing change of pace from the other kicks in the teeth I'd taken. Not like old Ace. He took it real hard. I ran into him in a bar a few years later and he bought me a beer, thinking he had a willing audience to hear him whine about lesbo-lap-licker-feminists. I told him to order me another while I went to the can, then slipped out the back door.

The thing that bothered me about Ellyn wasn't that she

displaced me, it was the way she went about it. She issued ultimatums about moving out all my stuff, she'd take my phone messages but not give them to Kadie, things like that.

"So, how is Ellyn?" I ask, not that I care.

"Well, you know we broke up, right? That was like six years ago."

I nod. The last time I ran into Kadie, I got the whole blow-by-blow. Kadie missed hanging out in bars and watching sporting events, which is something she and I used to do. Ellyn found that she missed being slapped around. At the time, each of them had taken up with new guys—Kadie with a ski instructor and Ellyn with a cop.

"Is Ellyn still going out with that cop?" I ask.

"Yeah, but not the same one. This guy's name is Zack. The last one's name was Jack. So she went from Jack to Zack."

"If this one doesn't pan out, she'll have to start back at the A's again," I say.

"Yeah, back to Ace." Kadie giggles. "Ellyn and I really don't see each other much anymore. But I'm on my way to see her now. She's having a birthday party for Zack. They live a few blocks from here." She rests her hand on top of mine, which is straddling the bottom of the window frame. "That was all pretty weird back then, you know, Phil?"

"Yeah, it sure was." I want to pull my hand away but I'm afraid I'll seem rude.

"What about you, Phil? I guess marriage is agreeing with you, huh?"

I nod. "Yeah, it's swell."

"You look great."

"I do? Thanks." I'd tell her the same thing, but she already knows it and I don't want her to have any doubts about my marriage. I slide my hand away. "Are you seeing anyone?"

"Uh-uh, not really. Dating's a real drag these days. You've practically got to exchange blood tests before you go to a movie. There's only so much you can do with a vibrator. I'm getting seriously horny."

I don't want to touch that line, and fortunately I don't have to. Kadie glances up to the next block, mutters, "Oh, shit," then starts off running. "Officer, officer!" she yells. "I'm just leaving."

She pauses at the corner and looks back at me. "I'll call you, Phil," she says. "We should get together for lunch."

I watch while Kadie persuades the parking vulture not to give her a ticket. Sex, I'm sure, has nothing to do with it. As she's pulling away, my car door opens and Frankie gets in.

"We're all set. We can pick him up anytime on Monday."

"Did you talk to the vet?"

"No, to the woman at the desk. But I made it clear exactly what we wanted." Frankie pulls a cigarette out of the pack on the console and lights it. "You'll never guess who was behind me on line in there." She doesn't give me time to guess. "Your pal Ron Ostrow."

Ron Ostrow once was a pal of mine; we were partners on an ambulance. But his status changed when I got booted off the fire department. I was never totally sure if it was intentional, but Ostrow played a crucial role in setting me up to get fired.

"Did you say anything to him?" I ask.

"Sure did. I said, 'Hi, you rotten piece of slime.' "

I don't have to ask Frankie whether she's telling the truth. If she doesn't like you, she lets you know. And she definitely doesn't like Ron Ostrow.

Neither do I, but I don't brood about him much anymore. I've got Frankie to do my brooding for me. I laugh and ask, "What did he say to you?"

"Nothing, he just stared straight ahead."

"He was probably afraid you'd claw his eyes out."

"I think he was more afraid you might be waiting outside and you'd beat the crap out of him. In fact, if we wait until he comes out, you could make him real nervous."

I put the car in gear and pull away. "Let's just go enjoy our weekend, sweetheart." Once I did beat the crap out of Ron Ostrow. It wasn't my finest hour.

Four

Frankie and I spend a delightful weekend in Wisconsin, our annual fall pilgrimage in search of fresh air, fresh apples, fresh beer and a fish fry. We find all four and don't give another thought to that cad Ron Ostrow or that cat Phull, except for Frankie pointing out that if our new vet, Dr. Nelson, adopted the old spray can, his name would be Phull Nelson.

Monday morning, it's back to the grind. Frankie heads for her office, which is about fifteen steps off the bedroom, and I head for mine, which is about fifteen blocks south of our house. Frankie needs an office, because she has real work to do. She used to be an investigative reporter for the *Sun-Times;* now she writes mystery novels about an investigative reporter for the *Sun-Times*. Her first book is coming out in a few months—it's called *Murder on Deadline*—and she's close to finishing her second. She still doesn't have a title for this one. That's one of the things I'm supposed to be working on in my free time.

The only reason I have an office is so I stay out of Frankie's hair. If we were home together all day, we wouldn't be married for long. Matter of fact, one of us would probably be dead.

Until a couple of years ago I had a job that was real interesting. I was a paramedic field officer for the Chicago Fire Department. I got to zoom around in an ambulance, run red lights and save people's lives. After Mayor Harold got elected, my job got more interesting. I got promoted to supervisor, which meant I got to zoom around in a fire chief's car, pick and choose which emergencies I wanted to respond to and oversee the guys who did my old job. I say "guys" because there were barely any women paramedics before Mayor Harold came into office. Until then, you pretty much had to be a Mick with a dick to get hired, though the occasional Pole with political clout could slip through the cracks now and then.

But then Mayor Harold died and about fifteen minutes later the city of Chicago canned my ass. Not because I did a bad job. That never stopped anybody from keeping a city job in Chicago. It's a long, sordid story and I won't regale you with the whole thing now. I don't usually tell it until after I've had a couple of drinks.

Basically what it came down to was this: I didn't kiss the right ass. Not only that, but I kissed the wrong ass. In the eyes of the guys whose asses I was supposed to be kissing, that's seen as kicking them right in the nuts. The Irish eyes of the boys in Bridgeport—that's the South Side neighborhood that runs Chicago—didn't exactly smile on a guy who supported a black for mayor over the son of Mayor Dick. Especially a guy who they figured was one of them. When they got their chance, they got me kicked out, but I managed to get in a few licks of my own.

It took some pretty fancy footwork, but I pocketed a handsome settlement. How handsome, you ask? Handsome enough that I don't have to worry about finding a job for a long time. That's a comfortable feeling, but as far as I'm concerned, it came at too high a price. I loved that damn job.

With this kind of financial freedom, I don't have the

slightest idea what I want to do. That's not true exactly. I've got lots of ideas. The problem is, they all sound good. For about a week, and then I get a new one.

I've thought about working at a hospital or teaching CPR. I tried both, in fact, but I gave up real fast. Working under fluorescent lights gives me a headache. I need to be out roaming around. I've thought about driving a cab, because I like to drive and I know the city, but that sounds like a good way to get shot or knifed and a bad way to make any money. I've thought about teaching school, but that sounds like a better way to get shot or knifed and a worse way to make any money. I've thought about offering my services as an accident investigator, but the only ones who'd hire me would be lawyers or insurance companies, and why in the world would I want to help them?

Lately I've been getting work as a paramedic on movies being filmed in Chicago. This sounds more glamorous than it is. If you've ever stood around watching a movie being made, you know what I mean. On a good day, I get to bandage Uma Thurman's boo-boos. On a typical one, I pass out ibuprofen to small-time actors with big egos and bigger hangovers.

Basically, I'm trapped in a luxurious sort of limbo, biding my time while I figure out what color my parachute really is. Most days I go to my office and take care of odds and ends. I do a lot of reading, listen to the radio, diddle with my investments, talk to friends, go to lunch, run errands. Some days I just drive around the city, watching people, thinking about things. One of these days, I just know it, some really great idea is going to walk up and bite me on the nose.

The arrangement that Frankie and I have calls for me to leave the house by nine-thirty each morning and stay away until at least three. By that time she's usually finished writing, and if she's not, I give her an excuse to stop. If she's having a bad day, which happens every so often, she can lay some of the blame off on me for interrupting her.

Unless I want Phull hanging out at the office, which I don't, there's no point in picking him up from the vet's until I'm on my way home. When I get to Purr & Bark, a couple of cars are playing cat and mouse with the last space in the lot, so I take the opportunity to barge through like a hog. Driving an ambulance gives you a sense of entitlement that tends to stay with you even when you're in a civilian vehicle.

Behind the outer door with the pastel paw prints, inside the small waiting room, I'm confronted by two mouth breathers and a drooler, and those are the pet owners. I move swiftly to the desk, which is manned by a stern-faced sixtyish woman with a silver braid stacked on her head and pink princess eyeglasses dangling from her neck on a chain. Her name is Madge, according to a badge that glimmers on her chest, catching the reflection from low-hanging fluorescents in a drop ceiling.

I think Madge may be trying to smile at me, but her dominant facial expression is an involuntary frown that has the effect of swallowing up any cheerfulness that may be lurking in the area. As she swivels in her chair and riffles through a file cabinet to her right, the frown becomes voluntary. She shakes her head and says she can't find Phull's chart.

This doesn't strike me as any cause for panic. Hospitals have been known to lose the charts of their patients, so why not vets' offices too? But Madge seems quite alarmed. I tell her about Phull's far-flung peeing prowess and suggest she might have found it necessary to put the file over by the heat vent to dry off.

That doesn't even raise a chuckle. Madge disappears into the backroom for at least five minutes. When she returns she's shaking her head and muttering, and there are two more customers with mutts on leashes behind me on line.

Madge doesn't acknowledge them or me. She plops back

down in her chair, swivels to a smaller file cabinet to her left, rests her glasses on her nose, pulls out a single sheet of paper, stares at it for about half a minute and lets out a long deep sigh.

"Just as I thought," she says.

"What's that?" I ask.

"Someone already picked up your cat."

"When?"

"This morning."

"Who?"

"How should I know?"

That catches me a little off-guard. I shrug. "Well, you work here."

"Mr. Moony, take a look around. It's hard enough to remember the pets. You can't expect me to remember the people who drop them off and pick them up."

I'm tempted to challenge Madge on this point, but I get the strong impression she's trying very hard to smile again. Plus I take her advice and glance at the five pets and owners waiting to see Dr. Nelson and realize that the parade of creatures through Purr & Bark could be one unmemorable, if colorful, blur.

"Let me get this straight," I say. "You're telling me that someone picked up my cat but you have no idea who?"

She puts up her hand. "You had the Maine coon, didn't you?"

"That's right."

"I seem to remember a woman dropping him off."

"Yes, that was my wife."

"Well, there's your answer."

"What's that?"

"She picked him up."

"No, she didn't."

"How do you know? Have you spoken to her?" Madge points at the phone on the counter, offering me its use, then turns her attention to the next customer, a white-haired mutt owner in a golf outfit. The owner has the white hair, the mutt's is brown. I wait until Madge is done done telling him it will be about fifteen minutes before responding.

"No, I haven't spoken to her. But I know that my—"

Madge gestures at the phone. "Call her. Couples like you get your signals crossed all the time."

"Couples like us?"

"You know what I mean."

I'm lacking whatever it takes to tell Madge I have no idea what she means. Instead, I call Frankie. It's my way of dealing with Madge—humor her by following instructions and call for backup at the same time. If Frankie were here, there'd be blood on the curtains by now.

"Honey, you didn't by any chance stop by Dr. Nelson's office and pick up Phull, did you?"

Frankie's dumbfounded by my question, but still manages to answer it with twice as many questions of her own, which is one of the ways she keeps people off-guard, especially me. "Why in the world would I have done that? Didn't you tell me you were going to do that?"

"Yes, I know; I did."

"Then why are you calling? Has something happened?"

"I'm just following orders from Madge."

"Who's that? What's going on, Phil?"

"She's the receptionist here. It seems that Phull's missing."

"Really? Is this our lucky day, or what?"

"No, I'm serious. Someone came in this morning and picked him up."

"I'll bet it's that creep Ron Ostrow."

"I think maybe you're being a little paranoid, honey." I don't tell her that's the first thought that flashed through my mind too.

Five

Once it's clear that the signals didn't get crossed on my end, the look of panic returns to Madge's face and she scampers to the backroom to fetch Dr. Nelson. Judging by all the scratching and sniffing and growling around me, I sense that the other customers are getting restless. Or maybe their curiosity has been aroused.

A moment later, Madge opens the door a crack and motions for me to join her. Immediately inside the door to my right, I find a short graying middle-aged man in a white lab smock and thick glasses.

"Mr. Moony." He holds out a soft wet hand. "Doctor Edwin Nelson. Madge has told me about the little mixup with your cat. I'm sure it's all just a misunderstanding."

"Which part do you think is a misunderstanding? Do you think someone took my cat by accident?"

"Uh, well, no. I mean I don't know. Are you sure someone didn't come in and pick up the cat for you—as a favor?"

"Dr. Nelson, I've already been over that with Madge."

Madge nods. "He called his wife, Dr. Nelson. I heard him."

"I see. Well, this is a very unsual situation for us. Frankly,

I'm shocked. Nothing like this has ever happened before."

It could be my imagination, but Madge looks surprised by Nelson's statement. I'm surprised by his next one.

"Now, Mr. Moony, as you can see, i've got a lot of customers waiting out front. I feel terrible inconveniencing you any further, but what I'd suggest is that you come back after six when we close. That way we could sit down and discuss the situation and determine how best to proceed. Would that be agreeable to you?"

A look of shock must flood over my face, because Nelson hastens to toss me a bone. "And naturally there'll be no charge for my services."

"Services? What services? Losing my cat? Do you call that a service?"

Nelson raises his hands, in a plea bargain. "Mr. Moony, please don't raise your voice. I don't need my customers hearing this."

"If anybody can barge in here and pick up someone else's pet, maybe they should hear it. Perhaps I should step back into the waiting room and let them all know."

"No, please, don't do that. Let's calm down and think this over a moment." Nelson lets out a long sigh and tugs at his beard. "Let's start back at the beginning. Now, you had the Maine coon, right? A male. That could be a very valuable cat to a breeder. Studs are in great demand."

"Phull wouldn't fill that bill. He's infertile."

"Phull?"

"That's the cat's name. His original name was Edwin. Just like yours."

"Oh, I see." He chuckles, but only a little. "Well, but a breeder wouldn't necessarily know he was infertile."

"He would after you neutered him. There'd be a bandage, right?"

Nelson shakes his head. "I didn't neuter him."

"Why not?"

"Because that wasn't requested."

"Yes, it was. That's why we brought him here. For you to fix him and check out his plumbing." I look at Madge.

"I remember your wife bringing him in, but I don't remember her saying anything about neutering him."

"You also don't remember who picked up my cat."

"I'm sorry, Mr. Moony. When you get to be my age, you forget things."

I start to offer an apology for the harshness of my tone, but Madge has something to add.

"You'll find out soon enough."

Apology withdrawn.

Nelson jumps back in. "I would have strongly discouraged neutering anyway, Mr. Moony. At his age, it could be a dangerous procedure. And why in the world would you neuter a cat that's infertile?"

"Because he slimes my house recreationally." That's as far into cat care as I care to get. "It looks to me like the most dangerous procedure around here is checking a pet into the place."

"Oh, come now, Mr. Moony. You can't expect us to check people's IDs. Besides, we know most of our customers. And the new ones, like you, come through referrals. By the way, who did refer you?"

"Mr. Ryan," Madge says, "Patrick Ryan." She actually works up a smile for me. "Such a nice gentleman."

I nod. "He's a prince." Then it's back to Nelson. "Do you have any customers who breed cats?"

"Mr. Moony, we have very good customers. I don't think any of them would steal your cat, if that's what you're thinking."

I glance at Madge. She looks a little less sure. "That *is* what I'm thinking, Doctor. Unless you can come up with another explanation."

Nelson tugs at his beard for a few moments. If Frankie were here, she'd ask if our cat had gotten his tongue.

"Any breeders?" I repeat.

"A few, yes. But not Maine coons, in particular. At least not that I'm aware of."

For an instant, Madge appears poised to say something, but she looks at Nelson and seems to think better of it. As I catch her eye, she shifts her glance down toward her feet. Only then do I notice that she's wearing furry slippers in a shade of long-forgotten pink. The slippers are adorned with cat's ears and whiskers. The eyes appear to have fallen off them, and the noses have been squashed into faded brown spots that look like mud or . . . well, let's leave it at mud.

"Would you care to give me their names?" I ask Nelson.

"I'm afraid that would be highly irregular."

"It's a highly irregular situation. I think that's something we all agree on."

Madge nods vigorously. So vigorously that her badge pinches her breast, turning her pursed little smile into a wince. Her lips quickly get in formation to pronounce the word "shit" but she stifles it. What comes out instead is a sound that vaguely resembles "meow."

I can't exactly put my finger on it, but there's something about forgetful old Madge that I rather like.

"Let me do this, Mr. Moony," Nelson says. "This evening, as soon as we close for business, I'll call those customers who I know to be cat breeders myself."

"And what are you going to ask them—whether they happened to take my cat home by mistake?"

"Frankly, I don't know what else I can do. Madge, are you sure you don't remember who picked up Mr. Moony's cat?"

"I'm sorry. You know how busy it is Monday mornings."

"Perhaps if you check your appointment book," I suggest. "Maybe that would jog your memory."

"Oh, heavens!" Madge slaps her forehead hard enough to knock her braid loose. "Now I remember why I don't re-member who picked up Mr. Moony's cat."

"Why's that?" Nelson and I both speak at the same time. We're finally in sync on something.

"Because I wasn't here this morning. I was at the podiatrist." She smiles sheepishly at me. "That's a foot doctor. I've got bunions something terrible."

"I know," I say. "About podiatry, that is. I'm sorry to hear about your bunions."

"Thank you. They're very painful."

"I'm sure they are. So who was working in your place at the front desk this morning?"

Madge looks at Nelson. "It was Abby."

"Oh, that's right." The vet nods.

"Well, let's talk to Abby," I say. "Is she still here?"

"No, she left the second I came in." Madge sounds a bit peeved. "Didn't even give me a chance to get my slippers on."

"Can you call her?"

I'm asking Madge, thinking she just might give Abby a good going-over, but Nelson's the one who shakes his head.

"No, she's not available right now. I'll talk to her this evening, as soon as I get home."

Madge excuses herself for a moment and goes back out the door to the front room. As it opens, we're greeted by a rowdy chorus of barking and snorting. If I were Nelson, I'd opt for a soundproof door too.

"How do you know Abby's not available?"

"She's my wife," Nelson says.

That doesn't fully answer my question, but I'm willing to assume he means he knows where she is at this moment and it's not near a phone.

The barking and snorting resumes for a moment as Madge returns carrying a large appointment book. "It's a zoo out there, Dr. Nelson," she says. "Since you can't reach Abby, I thought you might want to have a look through the register to see who was here this morning."

"I certainly would." As I lean in for a look, Nelson covers the page with his hand.

"I can't allow you to do that, Mr. Moony. The privacy laws as they relate to the small businessman are very strict these days."

"I imagine the liability laws relating to the disappearance of someone's pet are pretty clear too."

"Let's not start talking legality, Mr. Moony. I don't think either of us wants that. I promise you, I'll do my best to look into this as soon as we close for business."

For the moment, that sounds fair enough. Besides, I'm not making any headway hanging around there. But I do have one more question.

"By the way. Ron Ostrow. Is he one of your good customers?"

"Mr. Ostrow?" The name seems to give Nelson pause, and I don't think it's because he's trying to place it. "Why, yes. He's a good customer. He has two Dobermans. Why do you ask?"

"Heidi and Greta," Madge says.

"Do you know if he was here this morning?"

She shakes her head. "No, Friday. He picked them up on Friday."

"Mr. Moony, I really can't have you asking questions about all of our customers. I promise you, I'll speak to my wife this evening and call you tomorrow morning."

"This evening," I say. "Call me this evening."

Nelson sighs. "It could be late."

"Don't worry about it. I'm a real night owl. And so's my wife."

Six

I head up Milwaukee Avenue to Northwest Highway. Unless he's moved in the last couple of years, I know where Ron Ostrow lives. I doubt he's moved. Guys on the fire department, like all city employees, are required to live in Chicago. Most of them live as far from downtown as possible. Ostrow's neighborhood, Edison Park, is as far northwest as you can go and still be in the city limits. It's right on the border of Park Ridge, the town that prides itself on giving our nation first lady Hillary Clinton.

You're probably wondering why I'm so suspicious of Ron Ostrow. Basically, we're mortal enemies. How we came to be that way is a long story.

It starts the night I met Frankie, which is a story in itself. I was out to dinner with a buddy, Jack Egan, at a restaurant in the West Loop before taking in a hockey game. This was before the West Loop got redeveloped, before Chicago Stadium was torn down and reborn as the United Center, before Oprah gave birth to her TV studio, before Mayor Dickie got into office and started handing out tax breaks to his developer pals.

It was a 911 spot, the kind of place where the health-conscious eater orders the queen cut instead of the king and your choice of vegetable is baked or fries.

I noticed Frankie the moment she came in. She stood out a bit simply because she was an attractive woman. She stood out more because she was an attractive woman in a roomful of heart attacks waiting to happen. She stood out even more because she was an attractive woman out with a guy twice her age.

Jack and I were leaving when I heard the guy start to choke. Before that registered enough to make me react, I heard his dining partner cry, "Albie!"

I turned to see Albie standing up, clutching at his throat. He had THE LOOK on his face, the universal expression people get when they can't breathe—open mouth, purple complexion, bulging eyes. It goes in stages, from initial discomfort to controlled panic to abject terror to fear of God. As I moved toward Albie, he was about to enter stage three.

"Stand back," I called out firmly but calmly. It's a tone that almost everyone obeys. Even if you're not wearing a uniform.

I moved slowly, pausing for a pair of overweight gapers to make way. Paramedics are trained not to rush. Some people wonder why we don't run to an accident scene. They figure every second is precious and you can't afford to waste one. That may sound sensible but it's really not. Act too hastily and you increase your chance of screwing up. You also increase your chance of creating panic. Panic is contagious. If you convey even the slightest sense of it, a whole accident scene can go up for grabs. I've seen it happen. It ain't pretty.

I told Albie he was going to be fine. As soon as I did, you could see the relief spread over his face. He trusted me. Guys in his situation always do. They don't have any choice.

I moved behind him and told him to lift his arms as I spread mine around him. I clasped my hands together to make a single fist, lifted them to about his shoulders, then brought them down sure and solid against his diaphragm, lifting as they hit.

It was a piece of cake.

Piece of beef, actually. I didn't see it exit his mouth, but I felt the blockage give way on impact. Jack told me it landed three tables away.

Albie pulled free from me right away. I figured him for a guy who doesn't like another guy's paws touching his Armani, the kind of guy whose sense of relief to be breathing again barely outweighs his sense of embarrassment about being seen in such a vulnerable position. But I had Albie figured wrong. He wheeled, grinned and smothered me in a hug. He thanked me and thanked me and asked how he could ever repay me. Then he planted a kiss on each cheek, just like they do in the *Godfather* movies. For a moment, I wondered if he was going to introduce me to everyone as a friend of the family, but I later found out he was an old-time newspaper man. Instead he introduced me to his date, who turned out to be his daughter, Francesca. That turned out to be all the repayment I'd ever need.

She hugged me too and laid a soft one right on my mouth. The next day, she called to thank me again and invited me to lunch. I was surprised she'd been able to find my number, because I doubted she'd been listening when I'd told Albie my name. I soon learned that when it comes to details, Frankie doesn't miss much.

She'd never met a paramedic before, I'd never met a reporter. When I learned her last name, I realized she was the daughter of one of the best. She wasn't too shabby herself.

At the time we met, Frankie was starting on a long series about the Democratic Machine. This was during Mayor Jayne's last months in office. She had gotten into City Hall a few years earlier on a fluke. A huge blizzard that winter had crippled the city, and the place went up for grabs. The streets didn't get plowed, the garbage didn't get picked up, people shot each other over parking spaces. For years, Chicago had been known as THE CITY THAT WORKS. That was largely a myth manufactured by the Machine, but it was a myth most people believed, as long as the city was working for them. Some people still believe it, mostly people with city jobs or city pensions.

Mayor Jayne's election was big news, with the national media reporting that Chicago's mighty Machine had been toppled. It was bigger news that the person who did the toppling was a wisp of a woman. Few noticed her resemblance to the wicked wisp of the west.

Reports of the Machine's death were greatly exaggerated. Mayor Jayne had ranted about an "evil cabal" that was ruining the city, but she soon began cutting deals with the top caballeros. Many of the long-time hacks resented her, but it was business as usual.

You may be wondering what the Machine has to do with me and Ron Ostrow. The answer: everything. The Machine has always held power over people in Chicago. It holds power in lots of ways but mostly through jobs. The Machine gives jobs and it takes them away. I know all about this. I had it both ways.

I got my job through my alderman. I got to him through a friend of my mother's, Mary McGuire. Her son Roddy was a precinct captain in the 41st Ward. I went to Roddy, he went to the alderman. A week later he came back and said, "Come to Bingo at St. Pascal's on Friday night. Be ready to lose five hundred."

I was and I did, and I didn't even have to stay for the game. I just passed an envelope to a guy named Billy who was next to Roddy in the vestibule. When we got outside, I passed an envelope with $50 to Roddy. He didn't show any reaction. I never knew if it was too much or too little or just right.

I told this and other stories to Frankie. I also put her on to some other guys. Not just guys on the fire department, but cops as well. They all had stories to tell, and most of the stories fit right into the big one she was working on.

I didn't become Frankie's whistleblower for purely selfless reasons. I had my own axe to grind. I could see I didn't stand a chance of getting promoted. Most of the guys who talked to her felt the same way. But I had an ulterior motive: I very much wanted Frankie to like me.

When her exposé ran, the Machine took it on the chops and Mayor Jayne took it on both chins. Frankie showed how tests for police sergeant were rigged so that only guys with clout got picked, how the city altered crime statistics to make it look like violent crimes and arson were decreasing, how contracts were traded for campaign contributions, why it was almost impossible for blacks and women to get promoted. It wasn't that there was one single shocking revelation. It's just that, when you stacked them all up, it looked like the system was only working for a fortunate few.

Frankie's story wouldn't have made such a splash if there hadn't been an election coming up. It turned out to be a big election, the one that put Mayor Harold into office, the one that really did topple the Machine. It wasn't easy, and it wasn't pretty. In fact, it was downright ugly.

Before Mayor Harold, Chicago never had a black mayor. The only time we came close was in '76 when Mayor Dick died. The law of succession was so vague that it looked like a token black Machine alderman was in line to be interim mayor. But the city council went into emergency session and rewrote the law so that a white guy could be appointed instead.

The only reason Mayor Harold had a shot to get elected was because of a personal feud inside the Machine. The son of Mayor Dick decided to challenge Mayor Jayne for the Democratic nomination. Since she had been an adviser to his father way back when, it was like a spoiled nephew going at it with his crotchety aunt. They spent the campaign sniping at each other, leaving Harold to talk about how corrupt the whole system was. While bashing the Machine, Harold frequently quoted from a newspaper series written by one Frankie Martin. Frankie's father came out of retirement to be Harold's media adviser. That meant Frankie had to stop covering politics. She said it was a small price to pay.

The day of the primary saw the highest voter turnout in city history. Most of the white voters opted for one of the two white candidates. They split the white vote right down the middle, leaving the black votes for Harold. As Albie had predicted on TV the night before, that was almost enough to win the nomination. But the votes that put him over the top were from the few white voters who crossed over racial lines.

Honkies for Harold. I was one of them.

It was Frankie who convinced me to do it. She and what I saw during the campaign. At work there was a huge rift. Black guys were for Harold, white guys were against him. You didn't dare talk about it. I made that mistake with Ron Ostrow over a beer. I pointed out to him that Harold seemed a lot smarter than the other two. He'd been in Washington as a congressman, so he had a wider perspective. Dick and Jayne sounded like they'd never left their neighborhoods.

Ron agreed. But to him that was even more reason to vote against Harold. "You know what they say," he said. "The only thing worse than a dumb nigger's a smart nigger."

He was dead serious. I'd never heard the guy talk like that.

The more it looked like Harold had a chance, the more tense things got. On the street, blacks I'd just helped would mouth off, telling me my white ass was out of a job as soon as Harold got elected. If you were white and wore a Harold button, watch out. People would scream at you from passing cars. Not just men, women and kids too. I got jumped by two guys in a tavern where I was a something of a regular. The bartender called the cops and blamed it on me. Luckily, the cop who answered the call was a black guy.

I found another bar, and wore that button as a badge of honor. Past primary day and right up to the general election six weeks later. That's when things really got ugly.

For decades whoever won the Democratic primary was a shoo-in for mayor. A Republican has about as much chance of being elected in Chicago as a mass murderer. Until Harold won the primary. All of a sudden, Democrats who'd always done exactly what their precinct captain told them to do began taking an interest in "issues." At least that's what they told the pollsters. Brochures were printed saying Harold was a child molester. Some of the people handing them out were Democratic precinct captains. Democratic aldermen told their constituents to vote for the stooge that the Republicans were putting up. His campaign slogan had an urgent ring to it: BERNIE—BEFORE IT'S TOO LATE.

Harold barely managed to squeak into office. In his acceptance speech, he declared the Machine D.O.A. and gave credit to Frankie for putting the first nail in the coffin. Which meant that she also got a lot of the blame.

The obscene phone calls and death threats lasted for months. Changing numbers didn't help. At work, I got more than my share of credit and blame. I seemed to have quite a few new friends and just as many enemies. Some days, it was hard to tell them apart.

After Mayor Harold got into office, the El trains still ran, the garbage still got picked up. Harold himself had gotten his start through the Machine, back when the ward bosses had decided they needed a few blacks to represent all-black wards. So he knew how the system operated, he had been part of it. Except for the fact that the mayor was black and could put together two sentences without losing his train of thought, it was still the same old city that worked. It just worked for a few more people, and maybe a little better. After a while, it should have been hard to imagine what all the hostility had been about. But it didn't go away.

It continued through Mayor Harold's first term, when the

white aldermen on the city council used their majority to block every piece of legislation he introduced. It carried over into his reelection campaign, when Democratic leaders like Dan Rostenkowski still refused to endorse him. It continued right up to the moment he suffered a massive heart attack on the day before Thanksgiving. It even continued after that, though most politicians were so giddy about his unexpected departure that they suddenly couldn't find enough nice things to say about him.

To this day, there's still a rumor circulating that Mayor Harold was wearing women's panties when he died. He wasn't. A pal of mine is one of the guys who did CPR on him. But that just goes to show how the hostility never went away. Which finally brings me to how I lost my job and why I despise Ron Ostrow.

Seven

It was two years after Mayor Harold's death, right after Mayor Dickie got elected. It's not like he had anything to do with it. But once he was in office and the Machine was back in control, a lot of guys saw it as a time to settle old scores.

Ron Ostrow turned out to be one of them. He knew where to buy pot and he used to sell it to me and some of the other guys. It was no big deal, just small quantities.

As for me, I rarely smoke the stuff. I wouldn't smoke it at all if it weren't for my wife. And I certainly wouldn't buy it.

Ron told me he was planning to get some, so I put in an order for a quarter ounce. On the day he was supposed to get it, he called in sick. He called me to ask if I'd make the pickup for both of us.

Half an ounce of marijuana. That's like a dozen joints. I didn't think anything of it.

Ron told me to go to a gray stone two-flat on Sedgwick in Old Town. Nice building, nice neighborhood, right in my territory. I was a field supervisor, so I worked alone in a sedan instead of on an ambulance. I didn't have to answer any calls that required less than three ambulances. Ron had already paid the guy, so all I had to do was pick up a manila inside the door. I was out of my car for less than a minute. The cops were waiting by it when I got back.

Two plainclothes creeps. One of them I vaguely knew. His first name was George, I didn't know his last. He gave me a wise-guy smile and asked what I had in the envelope. I gave him a look like, "You've got to be kidding." When I asked if he was, his partner pulled out his service revolver and ordered me to hand it over and put my hands up.

I was so pissed off I was shaking. I wasn't scared, just mad. If you get caught with half an ounce of pot, you don't lose your job, you get a warning. There's a lot of crap you have to go through, like attending some Mickey Mouse seminar on drug abuse and undergoing urine testing. But you don't lose your job. If they fired every fire department guy who smoked pot, the city would go up in flames. The guys in charge all know it.

"So, Phil, tell me," George said. "What were you planning to do with all this cocaine?"

"Cocaine? Real funny, George." I gave him a wise-guy smile.

"Funny? I don't see anything funny." He turned to his partner. "Do you see anything funny, Ed?"

Ed shook his head. "Nope. Not a bit."

George looked back into the envelope. "Looks to me like there's at least two grams here, Phil."

"What! Let me see that!" I reached for the envelope, but George pulled it away. I still thought it might be a joke until Ed shoved me against the car and went into his Miranda monologue.

George grinned. "Gee, Phil, with all this coke here and you being so close to that school over there, looks to me like you're in some real deep shit."

My knees went weak. A few weeks earlier, the legislature had passed a law making it a felony to possess drugs within five hundred yards of a school. I could barely summon the strength to glance over my shoulder at the elementary school across the street. I didn't waste the strength I had left telling them what I thought of them. Not even when Ed said, "Too bad you don't have any nigger friends down at City Hall to help you out."

They hauled me in and booked me, charges on top of charges. Most of them were dropped quickly, all of them were dropped eventually. I was dropped from the fire department permanently.

It was front-page news for two days running. I was identified as "son-in-law of former mayoral adviser Albie Martin" and "husband of reporter Francesca Martin." The whole thing was clearly intended to embarrass them. And it did. Especially Albie.

I doubt the people who orchestrated it realized Albie had cancer. Even if they did, I doubt that would have stopped them.

I never found out exactly who set me up. Ron Ostrow swore he had nothing to do with it. But a pal of mine overheard him boasting to a supervisor that he'd played a role in getting me nailed. It could be that Ron was just taking advantage of an opportunity to kiss some ass. When I confronted him, he denied setting me up or boasting about it, and he continued to deny it even when I was knocking the piss out of him. He said it was the first time he'd ever bought dope from the guy. He didn't know his last name, but he'd met him through Dwayne Sutcliffe.

Sutcliffe was a field supervisor who had a black belt in karate and made sure everyone knew it. I always suspected he spent his weekends wearing a sheet over his head. I never got a chance to confront him. Two weeks after it happened, he was shot to death by a sixteen-year-old Puerto Rican kid in a traffic altercation near Humboldt Park. That made the front page too. He got a hero's sendoff, I got a bum rap. But at least I'm still here.

Frankie told me an old newspaper maxim that her father used to tell her: THE NEXT DAY THEY WRAP FISH IN IT. She said it's told to young reporters so they don't take themselves too seriously. She was telling it to me so I'd have the comfort of knowing I wouldn't be lunch for every radio call-in moron for long.

She was right. Although it seemed as if everyone knew who I was when it happened, I was old news by the time Dwayne Sutcliffe got shot. But to this day, some people still remember, strangers who buy me a beer at a bar or give me a long cold stare in the supermarket.

The section of Chicago where Ron Ostrow lives is a series of streets whose names, like Ron's, all begin with the letter O. As I'm confronted by the street signs—Osceola, Oconto, Octavia—I'm beginning to have doubts that I'll remember which O Street Ron chose to live and die on. Ron was one of those guys who liked to proclaim his intention to die right there in that house before he moved again.

I had been at the place only two or three times, and that was a few years back, and on nights when I was dropping Ron off after too much drinking. By both of us. In those days, if you got stopped by a cop while driving with a carload of guys named Bud Weiser and Johnny Walker, all you had to do was show your ID and he'd let you off with a stern warning: Have a nice night, drive home safely. I'm told things have tightened up since then, but you know lots of cops are still pretty loose with the guys they're tight with.

I recognize the street name as soon as I see the sign—Oriole. I now recall that Ron thought it was a funny coincidence that his wife originally was from Baltimore. This gave him a second reason to call her his little birdie. The first was her name, Robin. I thought the nickname fit because of her oversize beak and skill at henpecking. But the "little" part was wishful thinking. Robin had a much larger wing span than Ron.

I'm not as confident I'll be able to determine which house

is Ostrow's. The block, like so many in Chicago, is a series of identical pale brick bungalows fronted by curbside trees that die in a year and get replaced every three or four, depending on how well your alderman plays ball with City Hall. Whether it's a problem of bad soil or bad trees provided by a politically connected nursery, I don't know. With lot sizes close in dimension to cemetery plots, the houses call to mind tombstones.

I drive at a crawl, hoping for something that might be a helpful marker. Two thirds of the way down the block, I spot the best marking of all, Ron himself.

Ron is not alone. He's playing baseball with his two sons, whose names I either cannot now remember or never knew. My guess is that they're now about ten and twelve. Ron is not so much playing as coaching, urging them to get down on the ball and never take their eye off it. He's doing it so intently that he doesn't notice me pull up at the curb.

This gives me a moment to decide how I should play it. Ron is basically a chickenshit. I once did smack him around pretty good and you can be sure he hasn't forgotten it. Which means I could intimidate him by playing the tough guy. But that made me feel pretty small, and I know I'd feel even smaller repeating the scene in front of his sons. Even if Ron did take Phull, I'm not sure it would be worth that. Then again, I'm not sure it wouldn't.

I now notice that Ron's sons are not the only family members out in the yard with him. His daughters are there too. They're actually not his daughters. They belong to Robin. The time I met her, she told me that she'd always wanted daughters. When their two babies turned out to be boys, she decided to adopt two girls. A pair of Dobermans, Heidi and Greta.

I've never been a big dog fan. I've especially never been a big Doberman fan. An ex-girlfriend had one and I always refused to stay overnight because of him. "Don't be scared, Phil, he won't bite you," she used to reassure me. She didn't believe me when I'd say I was frightened just at the idea of being licked.

I decide to play it in a friendly matter. If the truth be told, the presence of Robin's girls has more to do with my decision than the presence of Ron's boys. But playing it friendly will be tricky, being I'm there because I'm openly suspicious of him. It's not like I'm coming to ask whether he happened to see Phull or if he noticed anything odd when he was at Nelson's office. I'm there because I think he's the schmuck who kidnapped my father's cat, only now I'm not so sure. Even if I don't trust my own instincts, I've learned to trust Frankie's. But she can also be rather headstrong, and suddenly it doesn't make a whole lot of sense that Ostrow would make off with Phull.

As I get out of my car, Ron glances my way. My timing isn't intentional so I can't take credit for it, but just at that moment one of this sons rifles a throw his way. The shock of seeing me causes Ron to commit a cardinal sin—taking his eye off the ball. The throw bounces off his glove, shoulder and head before rolling toward me. I make a point of getting down in front of the ball as I field it.

"Hello, Ron," I say as I toss it to him. I stay at the curb, beside the car, maybe twenty feet away.

"What the hell are you doing here, Moony?" Ron's got a new hairstyle, a buzzcut, and he's built more solidly than I remember. It could be he's put down the beer and picked up the weights.

I nod to indicate his two boys. "Can we talk privately for a moment, Ron?"

"No. We can't. I don't have anything to talk about with you, Moony." He turns and assumes a stance with his hands on hips—baseball glove on one, baseball in the other. I have a feeling he's thinking about winging it at me. I doubt he'd hit me if he did, but it would be hard to miss the LeBaron. I don't feel much of an attachment to the car, but I feel a very strong one for my father, who did.

"My cat is missing, Ron. I thought there was a chance you might have seen him."

"Yeah, I saw your lousy cat, Moony. At the vet's office on Friday, with your bitch wife."

"My what?" I'm trying to keep my cool, but the guy has just insulted my entire family. I take one step forward, he takes two back. This puts him about five away from the light pole where Heidi and Greta are leashed.

"You heard me. Your bitch wife." As if on cue, Robin appears at the front door. Even through the screen, I can see that she's added a few pounds since the time she downed four bratwurst in five minutes at a barbecue at my house.

"What's he doing here? Ronnie, you want me to call the cops?"

He waves her off. "Nah, I can handle it. He thinks I stole his dumb cat." He glares at me. "Isn't that what you're saying, Moony? That I stole your cat?"

It sounds dumb, even to me. So it must sound a whole lot dumber to them, coming out of left field.

I nod. "Something like that."

"You're crazy, Moony." Ostrow forces a loud laugh. He turns to his boys. "Ryan, Ralphie, take a look at this guy. He's crazy." He looks back at me. "What's wrong with you, Moony? Do you really think I'm stupid enough to snatch your cat?"

"I'm here, Ron. I wouldn't be if I didn't." I'm feeling sheepish and humiliated, but I do despise this guy, and someone did steal my cat.

"Well, I didn't. So get the hell off my property and don't come back!"

I'm back in the car before he finishes yelling. "I'm on my way, Ron. But if I find out you're lying, I'll be back."

As I slink away, I decide to let him have the last word. He's got lots of them. "Nobody cares about you anymore, Moony. They don't even remember who you were. You're a nobody, Moony."

Eight

When I get home, I can hear Frankie singing in the kitchen. That's a good sign. It means her work went well today. But it's not a good sound, because Frankie can't sing a lick. It's about the only thing she can't do well, and it's always puzzled me how such a horrible sound could come out of such a lovely face.

She stops as soon as I enter the room. She knows she can't sing, and she makes it a policy not to do so in front of anyone, including me. So the assault on my ears is short-lived, and there's plenty of sensory compensation available for my nose. Frankie's got a red sauce simmering on the stove. Next to her scent, that's my favorite smell on earth. Cooking is one of the things Frankie does very well, and no one does pasta any better.

"What's on the menu for tonight?" I ask.

"*Carciofi.*"

"Would that be asparagus?" Frankie's been trying to teach me Italian, and she figures the best place to start is food.

"Nope. Artichokes. But nice try. At least you knew it was a vegetable."

"So I get partial credit."

"Yup." She comes toward me and lays a kiss on my fore-head. "One little smacker and a glass of wine. But you have to pour it yourself."

"If you really expect me to learn, you're going to have to come up with stronger disincentives than that."

"Okay. No more sex until you learn all your irregular verbs. How does that sound?"

"Cold and lonely."

As I pour my wine, she asks for a full report on Phull. By the time I'm done, I've emptied three glasses and cleaned two plates. During pauses, she's vented her spleen plenty, mostly about Ron Ostrow.

"By the way," I say, "are you sure you made it clear to Madge that we wanted to have Phull fixed?"

"Madge is the gray-haired dump truck parked at the reception desk, right?" She lights her after-dinner cigarette and tosses one to me. This is the only time of day I smoke. "I just want to make sure I have this cast of characters straight."

"She's more like a bulldozer and closer to silver."

"There you go splitting hairs again." She smiles. Frankie always smiles after she's said something clever. "I'm positive I made it clear. I didn't come right out and use the word castration, but I definitely mentioned neutering. Why do you ask?"

"She said she has no memory of that."

"She wrote it down. I watched."

"Maybe she forgot where she wrote it."

"Oh, God. So you mean the little spray can still has his aerosol intact?"

"Evidently so."

"Well, at least that gives us some measure of revenge against the rat that snatched him."

"If that rat likes to breeds cats, that spraying business is music to his nose."

"That's right." Frankie shakes her head. "What a weird breed cat breeders must be."

"Speaking of weird breeds, I should call Pat." I collect our plates and Frankie follows me into the kitchen.

"Pat's not a weird breed, he's a rare breed," she says.

"Frankie, he's got four of the things."

"Yeah, you've got a point there."

Pat is busy changing litter boxes when he answers the phone. "Hello, stranger," he says, "I'm on the cordless." Pat never misses a chance to stick it to me for not staying in closer touch. There was a time, when times were tougher, when we talked every day. He's also the sort who's reluctant to try new technology; but once he does, raves about it.

Which means that he gives me a detailed review on how convenient it is to be able to be on the phone and change the litter box at the same time. Only he hasn't yet mastered the new skill of carrying on a phone conversation and changing the litter simultaneously. So I basically have to wait until he's done before he begins talking.

"So, what can I do for you?"

"I wanted to let you know that I took Phull to that vet you recommended—Dr. Nelson."

"Oh, yeah, Nelson, he's a good vet. What's the matter? Is the little guy sick?"

"No, just the usual. We—"

"You didn't take him in to have him fixed, did you?"

Uh-oh, I know where this is going. If I get Pat going on this subject, I'm in for a bigger going-over than I got from Ron Ostrow this afternoon.

"Because if you did," Pat continues, "I'm going to be very mad at you. I made it clear to Frankie that before you go and put that little guy under the knife, you better talk to me first. At his age—"

"Pat, Pat—listen to me." My tone makes Frankie wheel from her position at the dishwasher to see what's going on. "No," I say, "we didn't take him in to have him fixed."

Upon hearing this, Frankie realizes exactly what's going

on. She breaks into a grin and begins dancing in front of me.

"Are you sure about that?" Pat asks.

Frankie is now gesturing with her fingers and mouthing the words "LIAR! LIAR! LIAR! LIAR!"

"Yes, I'm sure." This is ridiculous. I'm forty years old and I'm lying to my dad and he's not even my dad.

"You wouldn't lie about that to me, would you?"

"No, Pat, I wouldn't lie to you," I lie. Frankie is now poking me with her fingers and continuing to lip-sync. I cover the mouthpiece with one hand and give her a shove with the other. "You get the hell out of here or I'll make you talk to him."

That stops her grin in an instant for an instant. "You wouldn't."

I nod. "I would."

She gets in two more pokes on me before she leaves, doubled over.

"Pat," I say, "all we did was take him to have his plumbing checked out. We left him there over the weekend."

"And how did he like the place?"

"I don't know. I haven't asked him."

"Very funny."

"I haven't had a chance to ask him yet. That's why I'm calling."

"What—you want me to stop by and pick him up? I'd be glad to do it."

"No, I already tried to pick him up. This afternoon. Strange thing, though. Someone else came in and picked him up before me."

"I don't understand. You mean someone you know?"

"No, I don't know who it was."

"Are you saying someone kidnapped Phull?"

"Catnapped, I think you'd call it. Yeah, that's how it looks."

"That's the craziest thing I ever heard. Did you talk to Madge—the lady at the desk?"

"Oh yeah, I talked to Madge all right."

"She's a piece of work, ain't she?" Pat chuckles. "So what did she say?"

"Lots of things. But the short of it is that she wasn't there this morning, so she doesn't know who picked him up."

"And you spoke to Nelson, I assume. What did he say?"

"He had lots of things to say too. None of them very helpful." I tell Pat about my futile attempts to see the register, Nelson's wife being at the desk, and his promise to call me after he spoke to her.

"Oh. Abby. She's supposed to be a real monster."

"How do you know that?"

"Madge told me. She said Abby treats her husband like dirt. And she's no help around the office. If I'm not mistaken, she also once mentioned that Abby breeds cats."

"Is that so? Maybe that's what Nelson was thinking about. He seemed to be holding something back on me."

"I'm not positive about that part, so don't quote me on it. Especially don't let that wife of yours quote me on it." Pat had been one of Frankie's best sources on her big story. He was the highest-ranking cop she'd talked to. "I'll drop by there and check with Madge tomorrow. I'll get us a look at the guest book, maybe a list of all the customers."

"Do you really think she'll let you do that?"

"Of course she will. I happen to command a lot of respect. Maybe you haven't noticed."

"Oh, I've noticed."

"Besides, I think Madge kind of likes me."

"I noticed that too. She was beaming when she mentioned your name."

"She mentioned my name? Why did she do that?"

"Nelson wanted to know who referred me."

52

"Oh, I see. I'll have a word with him too."

"Yeah, that would probably help. I'm sure he'd be more forthcoming with you than he was with me."

"Of course he would be. I'm one of Chicago's finest."

"You're a civilian now. You had a retirement dinner and everything, remember?"

"Makes no difference. Once the finest, always the finest. And there are a quite a few of us who take their pets there."

"Plus at least one fire department EMT."

"Oh yeah, who's that?"

It makes me feel sheepish all over again, but I tell Pat about my encounter with Ron Ostrow.

"Now that was a very dumb thing to do," he says when I finish. "You could've gotten hurt. He could've called the cops on you, he could've called his dogs on you. There's nothing good that could've come out of going up there loaded for bear like that."

I'm tempted to tell him I already know that, but Pat doesn't like to be interrupted when he's giving you a lecture. Besides, he heard me all the way out without interrupting. That's one of the best things about Pat. He may like to give lectures, but he's also willing to listen. He actually likes to listen.

"So the next time you think of doing something as dumb as that, you talk to me first, understand?"

"Yes, I understand. It was stupid and I won't do it again. And the thing that made it feel more stupid was that I realized, the moment I got there, that he wouldn't have taken Phull."

"Maybe he wouldn't've. But that don't mean he doesn't know somebody who would. I doubt the guy would have any trouble finding another guy who hates your guts as much as he does." He laughs. "And that would be just starting at random on the A's and just in his district."

"Thanks."

"Well, am I right or am I right?"

There's no need to answer that, but Pat likes it when you do, so I do.

"Ostrow presents an interesting angle to look into. I'll ask Madge about him too."

"You sure you don't mind doing all this?" There's no need to ask this question either, but I do just to be polite, if for nothing else. The fact is, Pat Ryan would cut his arm off for me. Another fact is, he's dying to investigate something. He'd probably cut his arm off for that too.

"Hell no, I don't mind. But I can't make it over there until noontime. Tomorrow's my morning to hang with the gang-bangers."

Pat is a charter volunteer for a program that aims to get rival gang members to sit down and talk to each other. He's had me down there a few times. Not as often as I said I'd come, and not, I now realize, for quite some time.

"How's that going these days?"

"Phil, don't get me started. Bunch of little pissants with guns, that's all they are. They could all use a good kick in the ass. But this program, it started out so successful that now everybody wants a piece of it. They've got some of these churches involved in it, they've got, like, three city agencies involved in it. Which means you've got a bunch of sancti-monious do-nothings and a bunch of so-called ministers hanging around trying to sound smart. And now you've got the Park District involved in it, and the schools involved in it, and some of the counselors think all they should have the kids doing is shooting hoops together...don't get me started."

"I think I already did."

"Well, then somebody better stop me before I start again. And if you won't, I will. You get off the damn phone and get into bed with that lovely wife of yours. Me, I'm going to turn on Letterman in time to catch the stupid pet tricks."

"Don't you have enough pet tricks going on right there in your apartment?"

"It's not for me that I'm turning it on, it's the cats. They love it."

I don't ask for details on how he can tell. I just ask what time he wants me to meet him at Purr & Bark.

"That's not necessary. I'll handle it myself and get back to you."

This surprises me a bit, because Pat usually likes having company. And disappoints, because I'd actually like to watch him in action working on Madge. And Nelson, for that matter. "You're sure you don't want me to come along?"

"No, it's okay. I'll call you tomorrow afternoon and let you know what I find out." Pat lets out a yawn. "By the way, you didn't call the coppers about Phull being snatched, did you?"

"No. And neither did Nelson."

"No, of course, he wouldn't."

"Should I have?"

"Are you kidding? They would've laughed you right off the line."

Pat laughs me right off the line just as Frankie, who's finally stopped, reenters the kitchen. She treats me to a sympathetic pat on the shoulder that evolves into a most welcome and, to my mind, hard-earned, backrub. "Wow, he sure was giving you a going-over. Good thing you didn't tell him we were thinking of having Phull put to sleep."

Her laughter resumes, my backrub ends.

"Next time," I say, "it's your turn to talk to him."

"Uh-uh, he's your cat."

"My father's cat."

"Same difference."

"Well, you're the one who wouldn't let Pat take the little squirt gun off our hands."

"Oh, come on. You knew how bad that would be for him. You wouldn't have permitted that either."

"Are you kidding? Sure, I would've."

"Really?"

"In a heartbeat."

"I see. So now this is all my fault."

"I'm willing to give you at least some of the credit."

"Well, thank you for sharing. So what did Pat propose we do?"

"He's going to start by having a talk with Madge."

"To what end? Is he going to recover her memory?"

"Nope. Just our cat, hopefully. He says she'll give him carte blanche—a look at the appointment book, the customer list."

"Really?"

"Pat's a cop. He has a way of getting people to talk. Especially silver-haired dump trucks. In the case of Madge, I think he'll resort to charm."

Frankie nods. "I imagine a little bit of Pat's charm would go a long way on Madge."

"I didn't tell you—she's already a little sweet on him."

"That makes sense. In that case, he could probably charm her right out of her slippers."

"Oh, did you get a look at those?"

She nods. "A look, and a whiff."

Nine

I wasn't being precise when I told Dr. Edwin Nelson that Frankie is a night owl. In fact, she's more like a bat. There's a quality of blind fury about her. It's a bluntness that I've noticed in most of her journalist friends. I've never known whether to attribute it to their calling or their drinking. In Frankie, it comes equipped with a precision radar system.

Anyway, she's the one who fields Nelson's phone call, which comes just at the start of the stupid pet-tricks segment, which we're watching on the bedroom TV. By the time she's done with him, I'm sure the guy is panting and on all fours.

Here's a snippet of Frankie's end of the conversation, just to give you an idea.

"Let me get this straight, Dr. Nelson. You're saying that you have no news about our cat because you've been unable to reach the person who checked the cat out of your place this morning, is that correct? And that person is your wife. Is that also correct? And you don't know, Dr. Nelson, where she is or when she's coming home. And now you're going to bed, so it isn't likely you'll have a chance to speak to her this evening, which means you won't have any news for us until tomorrow morning, and then only if your wife gets home in time for breakfast. Is that essentially what you wish to tell me?"

"Okay, then. We'll expect to hear from you tomorrow— in the morning, early."

"You forgot to wish him sweet dreams," I say when she hangs up.

She smiles and kisses me on the forehead. "I was saving that wish for you. I can't imagine how you're going to be able to get a good night's sleep, having it on your conscience that you lied to Pat about our cat."

"And I don't know how you're going to be able to wake up in the morning without that cat here to lift up his tail and wipe his butt across your face."

Somehow, we both manage.

Frankie is parked on the bed with a copy of the *Sun-Times* under her nose. A cup of coffee is parked on her night table. If I remember to say *"buon giorno"* instead of "good morning," she'll bring one for me too. This is the behavioral modification method of language instruction.

I do and she does.

"Any deaths I'll be happy to hear about in the paper this morning?" I ask. The obits are the first section that Frankie goes for.

"I haven't looked yet. This morning I started on the classifieds. Listen to this one: 'MAINE COONS—GUARANTEED: A MORE LOVING, LOYAL, LUSCIOUS BREED OF CAT YOU'LL NEVER FIND.' Luscious? What are you supposed to do with the thing—eat it? And if you're guaranteed never to find one, why would you go looking for it in the first place?"

Frankie has this habit of editing aloud all writing that appears in the newspaper. It's a habit that I find rather annoying, especially when I'm trying to read the box scores. I've called it to her attention, but she says she can't help it, it's an addiction.

" 'CALL ABBY FOR AN APPOINTMENT.' "

"Who? Let me see that." I take the newspaper from her

hands and read the ad. "It's a north suburban area code."

"Winnetka."

"How do you know that?"

"She told me when I called her."

"You called her? Why'd you do that?"

"It's the only ad that specifically mentions Maine coons. It could be such a specialized deal that there are only a few breeders in the whole area. I figured we'd at least be able to find out who they are."

"Do you want to know who I think this one is?"

"Who?"

"Nelson's wife. Her name's Abby. Pat said he thought she might be a cat breeder."

"You didn't tell me that."

"He told me not to tell anyone until he found out for sure."

"What—I'm just anyone?"

"I forgot. And I didn't have a chance to tell you, you were so busy giving her husband obedience lessons."

Frankie nods to indicate she'll concede me that point. But it's a grudging nod. "Isn't Abby the one who Madge says was at the desk yesterday morning?"

"Exactly."

Frankie chews on her lower lip. "It couldn't possibly be that simple, could it? The wife of the vet is stealing customers' cats?"

"I don't know. Maybe there aren't that many of this breed."

"It's pretty brazen. I don't think she'd be able to get away with it for too long."

"Maybe she's a cat klepto."

"Wow, talk about your strange breeds." She looks at the clock. "Our appointment is in two hours. I think we should make a point of getting there early."

"I think we should talk to Pat before we go over there and start asking questions."

"Who said anything about asking questions? I think we should just go up there, say we're looking for a cat, and have a look around. If we don't find Phull, there's nothing lost."

"And if we do find him?"

Frankie holds up her fingers and wiggles them. "If we do, I'll scratch her eyes out."

An hour later, after battling the reverse commuter traffic on the Edens Expressway, we're in Winnetka. It's a tidy little village right on Lake Michigan, fifteen miles north of downtown Chicago, a perfect model of fine, upscale suburban living. The low-end buy-in is at least three hundred grand, and that's for a tiny box with a view of the expressway and a whiff of the town dump. But people will pay anything to guarantee good schools and safety for their kids. One problem, though. Even in Winnetka, there are no guarantees.

Like a few years back, when a baby-sitter named Laurie Dann went off the deep end and shot up an elementary school. Or when a New Trier High School student named David Biro broke into a young couple's town house and shot them to death just for the hell of it.

When we get to the address that Frankie had been given, the name on the signpost at the end of the driveway confirms that the Abby in the classified ad is the dear wife of Dr. Nelson. Unless there are two Abby Nelsons in the cat-breeding racket.

The Nelson house is off Hill Road, which means I should probably be calling it an estate. The cobblestone driveway has more curves than a runway of supermodels, and it's a morning's drive from the wrought-iron gate to the marble-ized front steps.

"Nice shack," Frankie says, as she gets out of the LeBaron. "I'd say Doc Nelson is doing just fine for himself."

"Maybe there's a fortune to be made breeding gushers like Phull."

"I'm inclined to think it's her little hobby."

It takes two rings to get a response from the doorbell. It comes in the form of a female voice warbling through the intercom. Actually it sort of purrs, a measure of the sound quality of the intercom and the sleepiness of the tone.

"Yes, who is it?"

"Abby, I'm Frankie. I called on the phone about the cat."

"You're early, darling. We said ten-thirty."

"Oh, we did? I thought it was nine-thirty. I'm sorry."

"You'll have to wait a minute."

We end up waiting about five before the figure of a blond-haired woman appears on the staircase through the stained glass window in the arch of the door. When she opens the door, I see that it's quite an impressive figure. This observation doesn't require much calculation. Abby is clad in an overlapping, intersecting assortment of skintight pastels—leotard, leggings and other skimpy pieces made of materials like Lycra and nylon that I believe go by the fashion designation of "workout togs." Her tanned skin itself is so tightly wrapped that there's not a wrinkle visible at first glance and I don't want to take any more for fear that she, or Frankie, will think I'm staring.

But it's hard not to. Despite her magnificent physique, she can't hide the fact that she's fifty, and I'm being generous. She's tall and slender—legs, arms and torso—and has a small round face with tiny features. The overall package would look almost catlike, except for one, or perhaps I should say two, prominent features. She has a chest that's large enough to seat a full litter of kittens comfortably. At the moment it's occupied only by one big furry guy. And he does look comfortable.

"Abby," she says, extending her hand to Frankie. She angles toward me. "And you'd be her—husband?"

"Phil," I say. "Yes, that's right."

"You can never be too sure these days." She lets out a long dry chuckle. "And this is Bobo. He's not my husband. I just wish he was." She begins stroking Bobo's head and speaking in baby talk. "Yesh, my shweet boy, you'd be such a good catch, wouldn't you, yesh, you would."

Frankie and I both look to the staircase behind her, where, halfway up, is a guy in shorts, a tank top and bare feet. He's about half my age and twice my size and there's not an ounce of fat on him. He looks like he could bench-press the whole house.

Abby steps back and signals him to come down with a flick of her hand. "Oh, and this is Rod. He's my trainer. We were just having my workout. I find it quite invigorating to work up a good sweat in the morning, don't you?"

Frankie nods politely. The only sweat she ever works up in the morning is from using up all the hot water before I can get into the shower.

Rod moves to the bottom of the steps, stops stiffly and nods. From that distance, I can see that he also has worked up a sweat, though it might just be fallout from the dousing of mousse that has turned his blond locks into glistening strands or greasy strings, depending on your view of men's hairstyling. Me, I've always gone for the dry look.

"You can stay here, Rod." Abby takes a step outside and makes a sweeping gesture with her arm. "Follow the yellow brick road."

It's a path, actually, and it runs right along the front and side of the house before cutting away from a glassed-in porch in the back that appears to have every piece of exercise equipment ever advertised on late-night TV. From there it angles down a slope to a free-standing shed that is about the size of our entire house and needs far less exterior work.

Abby pauses at the door. "Okay, Bobo, you big shtud, we're going to see all your babies again, so act nice for the folks." She smiles at us and rolls her eyes. "He's such an animal."

The opening of the door is the first sign that things are not all trim and tidy inside the compound. Ventilation, or lack of it, is a big problem. If I had my choice between stepping inside and taking a punch in the nose, I'd have to go with the punch. Carpeting is another area of concern. It's white, plush and wall-to-wall. At least that's how it started out. I'm sure it's hard to keep it that way in a room that's wall-to-wall litter boxes and feeding bowls. The furnishings feature every variety of scratching post known to cat, and every perch on each one of them is presently being put to use.

"I've got two new litters, so it's a little bit crowded," Abby says, motioning for Frankie to go in. "Now, Bobo, shweetie, you remember to be a gentleman."

It takes Frankie a moment to work up the courage to step inside. I follow bravely behind Bobo and Abby, whose arms are showing goose bumps in the morning chill.

The three of us stand near the doorway, watching as Bobo saunters deliberately across the room, like a cop patrolling a bad neighborhood. One gaze around the room is all I need to tell me that Phull is not among the room's inhabitants, even though their population may number in the low three figures. Almost all of the cats before us are far smaller than Phull. The few that aren't are being pressed into service for that special kind of parenting duty that guys like Phull and Bobo aren't naturally equipped to handle.

"Do you know a lot about Maine coons?" Abby asks.

"Not really." Frankie is already on her way back out the door. "Just that they're loving, loyal and luscious."

"Oh yes, they—" It's not the fact that Frankies uses the word luscious that causes Abby to stop in mid-sentence and shoot her a questioning look. It's the way she says it, with sarcasm dripping off the word, much like the styling mousse that is probably still leaking from Rod's hair.

As Abby bends down to collect Bobo, she keeps her gaze fixed on Frankie. "You look familiar," she says as she rights herself. "Have we met before?"

"No, I don't think so." Frankie looks away.

"For some reason, you don't seem very interested in the cats."

"Those are all kittens. What about the older males? Do you keep all your studs over in the main house?" She nods toward the exercise room, where Rod is speeding in place on a cross-country ski device.

Abby frowns. "I don't understand. Are you looking for a cat or are you looking to breed them?"

"I don't know, I'm just starting out."

"Well, I've only got one stud, and you can't have him." She rubs Bobo's head. "Ishn't that right, shweetie?"

I think I gasp aloud. "You mean to tell me Bobo is the father of all those cats?"

Abby grins like a proud mother. "Pretty impressive, don't you think?"

"I'll say. But I suppose the females deserve some of the credit. He must have more wives than the Emir of Kuwait."

I think that one goes over Abby's head. Or maybe she's preoccupied with another subject.

"I know where I saw you! You came in when I was at the office on Friday afternoon. You're the people who lost their cat, aren't you?" Abby's voice is getting louder with each statement. "My husband told me all about you." She turns to me. "He told me all about how you who barged into the office and threatened him yesterday."

"Uh, that's not exactly what happened."

"Our cat wasn't lost," Frankie says. "He was catnapped. And it happened while some frosted blond bimbo was knocking her big bazungas around the front desk—you."

"That's it! I've had enough. You get off my property!" For a moment, I think Abby is about to let Bobo loose on Frankie, but instead she wheels and begins speed-walking back to the house. "Rod, Rod! Make them leave. Make these people leave."

She's setting a blistering pace. On a normal day, I'll bet

she does it with weights on her wrists. I have to break into my highest speed, an all-out jog, to catch up to her.

"Mrs. Nelson, yes, I admit it, we did come here because we suspected you. But now, after seeing Bobo, we realize that you had nothing to do with it. So if you'll just please tell us who picked him up yesterday, we can—

She halts and turns. "I don't remember and I wouldn't tell you if I did!"

Just then Rod steps out from a side door leading into the jungle gym. Abby moves over to stand beside him. The only thing that would make the scene play better is if Rod came swinging out on a rope.

"I do not like being accused of stealing someone's cat," she says. "And if I was interested in having your cat, which I wasn't, Miss Gutter Mouth, I wouldn't have stolen him. I would have inquired whether or not he was available." She turns to her trainer. "Rod, these people are upsetting me. Make them leave."

Rod's arms unfold methodically, and his hands settle on his hips. By the time they get there, I'm already three steps up the yellow brick path and wishing I were back in Kansas. His mouth opens slowly, as if he has to think about it first, and the sound that comes out is about three octaves higher than I expect. The effect is like a bicycle horn coming from a sixteen-wheeler.

"You heard the lady. You better leave."

Frankie, who has not given ground until now, smiles at him. "Of course, Rod, we're leaving right now. We'll let you two get back to your workout."

Ten

Unbelievable!" Frankie fumbles for her cigarettes as soon as we get in the car. "How many tummy tucks and face-lifts do you suppose one body can endure?"

"I think she may be into double-digits."

"Breast reduction—that's what she ought to be thinking about."

"But then there'd be nowhere for Bobo to live."

Frankie doesn't laugh. I wait until she's lit her second cigarette before speaking more seriously.

"I think you really blew that one, honey."

She stares straight ahead and smokes. With Frankie, a non-response like that is an admission of guilt. Which is exactly what I've been waiting to hear.

"But don't feel bad. Yesterday, I blew it with Ostrow. Today, you blew it with Abby."

"I made a damn fool out of myself."

"In front of Abby? I don't think you have to worry about it. But I do wonder what happened to that sense of reportorial restraint that you pride yourself on."

"I don't know. Something about her brought out the Sicilian in me."

"Oh, bologna! You just wish you had a nice set of workout togs like that." I can tell Frankie's really stewing because she doesn't congratulate me on my clever use of Italian.

"She must have paid close to five hundred dollars for that silly outfit."

"I think she probably feels it's important to look nice for Rod."

"She looks ridiculous. And I managed to let her make me look ridiculous. That's the bad part."

"But it wasn't a total loss. Now we at least know that she doesn't have Phull."

"What do you mean—how do we know that? I think maybe she does have him. Stashed away in one of the upstairs workout rooms."

"Uh-uh. Bobo would never allow that."

"Phil, I am not buying the idea that one cat produced all those kittens. That's the most disgusting thing I've ever heard. If that's true, I want to move to another planet."

"One where there's no men, I suppose."

"Naturally." She pounds her hand on the dashboard for emphasis. "What makes you so sure she didn't snatch our cat?"

"Because I think what she said made sense. If she was interested in Phull, she could have offered to buy him from us."

"We never would have sold Phull to her."

"Huh?" I turn my head to look at her and almost drive us off the road. "You mean if she had offered us five hundred or a thousand bucks, you wouldn't have said yes?"

She has to think that one over. Which amazes me.

"Frankie, only three days ago, we were ready to pay someone to toss Phull onto the big Hibachi." I stop for a moment. "Aren't you proud of me for using my Italian?"

What—hibachi? That's not Italian, that's Japanese."

"Okay, yeah, you're right, I got carried away. Let me try again. How about: 'Honey, only three days ago, we were ready to turn him into *felino al forno*" I can feel myself beaming. "How was that?"

She's practically beaming too as she slides over and plants a kiss on my cheek. "That was not bad. A couple of more years and you'll be ready to order for yourself."

"A couple of more minutes and I'll be ready to order myself a martini. Is it time yet?"

We have a standing agreement not to imbibe before noon. It's for the protection of both of us. I like to think it's mostly for Frankie's sake, she likes to think it's mostly for mine. Co-dependency can be a beautiful thing, if you play it right.

Frankie checks her watch. "We've still got fifteen minutes, but by the time we park and find a table and all . . ."

I pull into a tavern on Lake Avenue in Wilmette, the only bar in the north suburbs that I'm familiar with. Since it's a German place, I lower my sights to beer. Which is a wise decision. Daytime martinis, I've found, can be *molto pericoloso*.

After lunch, I drop Frankie back at the house and I head down to my office. She's planning to work, I'm planning to pretend to.

My office is right on Logan Square, where Milwaukee Avenue crosses Kedzie and Logan boulevards. When it was designed near the turn of the century, Chicago's boulevard system was modeled after the boulevards of Paris. But anyone today who thinks there's any resemblance probably has never been any farther from here than Paris, Illinois.

I picked the spot for three basic reasons: location, atmosphere, price.

Logan Square is only three stops down the Northwest El line from our neighborhood, Independence Park. When I first rented the place, I figured I'd ride the train during the winter and ride my bike during warm weather. So far, I've driven my car every day.

As far as atmosphere goes, I figure any neighborhood where you see *cerveza fría* signs hanging next door to places with names like Droszka Karzckma, you know things will never get too dull.

The building itself is an ancient three-story walk-up that once formed a perfect right triangle. The sagging legs of the triangle face Logan on the north and Kedzie on the west. The hypotenuse parallels Milwaukee and runs the length of the alley behind the Banco Popular de Puerto Rico. The tip of the triangle points directly to Logan Square, which is actually a circle. At the center of the circle is a four-sided marble stairway leading to the Illinois Centennial Monument, a towering white obelisk that isn't as tall as the Washington Monument in D.C., but is impressive just the same.

At the top of the obelisk sits an American eagle. At the bottom of it, on most afternoons and evenings, sit groups of teenagers. I've heard them refer to the monument as "the turkey." I don't think many of them are headed for college.

Of all the tenants in the building, I've got the best seat in the house—a top-floor cubicle on the point of the triangle overlooking the park. By standing on my desk, I'm almost eye to eye with the eagle. By bending down low, I can see half a block up Milwaukee Avenue, past the blood bank, the liquor store, and the billboard with an 800 number for getting in touch with the Virgin Mary, to a clothing store that offers "styles to fit your wallet."

In addition to the great view, the two windows provide cross-ventilation, which is a plus in the summer. There's no air-conditioning, so the only relief from the heat comes from portable fans. I've got three of them. It took some doing, but I've learned how to adjust them to neutralize the fumes from Ronnie's Grill, the twenty-four-hour greasy spoon on the ground floor. On really hot afternoons, when the sun turns the building into a Dutch oven, I've been known to slip out to the Mexican place across the square and siesta on margaritas.

All this for the unbelievably low price of $275 a month. My landlord, Jerry, hasn't raised the rent, and promises he won't until he's finished rehabbing the building. I figure I'm set for the next ten years. Jerry has big plans, but he comes up short on the follow-through. He says I'm his best tenant, which isn't saying a whole lot.

On the ground floor, there's a dry cleaner called Ruby's that's no longer owned by Ruby and a newspaper shop that still carries *Look* magazine. Jerry was thrilled when the beeper store gave way to a coffee boutique, but I don't think they're going to get off the ground. On the second floor is a Polish podiatrist whose name I can't pronounce. His sign has a translation underneath for those who are confused by long words: FOOTS DOCTOR. Next to him is a psychic reader named Madame Yvetta. Our paths have never crossed, but I've heard she's very accomplished at what she does. Or at least what she did for an elder statesman of the block who hangs out at Ronnie's and never leaves home without his Notre Dame cap. While buying coffee one morning, I overheard him telling one of the waitresses that she had put him in contact with the spirit of Knute Rockne. Rockne grew up in this neighborhood.

There are a few other tenants on the second floor, but I don't have a clue what they do. I suspect they either like it that way or have something to hide. I should talk. I doubt anyone has any idea what goes on behind the frosted glass door up on the top floor with the hand-lettered sign MOONY ENTERPRISES—WORLD HEADQUARTERS. I imagine anybody who has seen it thinks it has something to do with the Reverend Sun Myung Moon. They probably flee when they hear my footsteps, afraid that I'll start hustling them to buy flowers.

I park the LeBaron outside the Norwegian church where Knute Rockne once served as an altar boy. As I stroll across the square, past the boys killing time under the turkey, I'm staring in the face of what is often my biggest decision of the day: whether to drop a buck and change on the coffee of the day at the new place or half a buck on the coffee from yesterday at old Ronnie's. With the sun shining, the breeze blowing, the leaves swirling and a mild beer buzz going inside my head, everything should seem right with the world right now. And it almost does, except for this gnawing need to find the damn cat I've been trying get rid of.

Eleven

The phone is ringing as I face the challenge of unlocking the office door without spilling my cappuccino. What can I say—I'm a yuppie at heart.

I get to the phone before the answering machine engages. The voice on the line is familiar, I have no trouble placing it.

"I love this damn Internet," Frankie says.

"I take it you haven't started working on your book."

"No, dear, I'm still waiting for you to come up with a title."

"How about *Final Edition?*"

"Hmm." I can picture her chewing her lip. "You know, that's not bad."

"You're going in circles, sweetheart. When I suggested it three weeks ago, you said you didn't like it. 'Sucks' is the word I think you used."

"Yeah, I guess you're right, it does suck. So anyway, I figured you'd be dying to know what I found out."

"I didn't even know I was waiting for something."

"Our friend, Dr. Nelson. Purr & Bark is the third vet office he's had. He has this curious habit of filing for bankruptcy. It looks like he likes to roll over, play dead and come back to life. He's done it twice. First in New Jersey, then in Ohio."

"It sounds like he's on his way to California."

"With a pack of pissed-off creditors snapping at his tail. Aside from them, there seems to be this other problem: He loses people's cats."

"Is that right?"

"Yup. I found two instances in New Jersey, four in Ohio. Nothing in Chicago, but it's probably not big enough news to make the papers here. I'm going to check with the state vet board and find out if there've been any complaints registered against him in Illinois. He's been here for at least four years now. The only reference in the Chicago papers I could find was a photo of him and the missus at a benefit ball for the zoo. You should see the slutty dress she was wearing."

"You found all that out in the time it took for me to get here?"

"I told you, I love this Internet. Just think, if you could figure out how to set up your E-mail, I could zap all these lovely files over to you right now and you could read them for yourself."

"But, darling, I find it far more pleasurable to hear it through your lovely voice." Which is the truth. But it's also true that I wouldn't mind being able to have a look at Abby Nelson's dress.

"In the two cases in New Jersey, the cats were missing for a while—I don't know how long—but then they suddenly showed up. In Ohio, when the owners came to pick up their cats, they were told that they'd died. They were given urns with ashes in them. Nelson cremated their cats before telling them that they were dead."

"Which makes you wonder whether the cats they cremated were the same ones they said were dead. When our cat Hank died, we got him cremated. The jar is sealed. You have no way of knowing whose ashes are in there—or even if they are ashes."

"Right. You just trust that your vet is honest."

"Which in this case we do have to wonder about. Now is Abby mentioned in any of these stories, or is it all just Edwin?"

"Good question. She comes up in two of them. And it sounds like she's the one who took in the cats. And that doesn't mean she wasn't involved in the others. It's just that she wasn't mentioned."

"So maybe she is a cat klepto, after all."

"Or maybe just a Maine coon snatcher. At least one of the missing cats was that breed. The other stories didn't specify the breed. By the way, did you know that the Maine coon is the only natural breed of domestic feline in North America?"

"What does that mean?"

"It bred in the wild. You didn't have a bunch of guys in lab coats like Dr. Nelson working on developing it. It was also the first show cat. Then it fell into disfavor for a few decades. People who showed their cats started moving into more exotic breeds. But it made sort of a comeback in the sixties."

"Oh, those sixties."

"When everything went back to natural again for a while."

"And you just learned all this."

"Surfing the net, baby." Frankie pauses, and I can hear her lighting a cigarette. "Now, back to Nelson. Do you have any theories on why in some cases the cats disappeared and came back and in others they were said to have died?"

"Frankie, you're moving a little fast for me. I've had my head full just trying to digest this information. I haven't really had time to form any theories." But as I tell her that, one begins to form. "You know, as a matter of fact, I do have a thought."

74

"Well, tell me, please."

"What if, in Ohio, when they were reported dead, they were all female cats? Abby was swiping them and bringing them home to be swept off their feet by Bobo or whoever she had playing the role of the Big Bopper back then. She kept them to be part of his lair."

"Ooh, icky. And in New Jersey?"

"In those cases, how about if she was snatching male cats and collecting their sperm?"

"Ooh, ickier." She takes a very deep breath. "Phil, I think I've had enough cat chat for a while. I'm going to get to work."

As soon as we hang up, it occurs to me that my theory might be wrong. I have a feeling Bobo could be one of the cats that might have been snatched in Ohio. I think about calling Frankie back to tell her, but she seems to have beaten me to it.

I pick up the phone on the first ring. "Yes, darling. What else did you find out?"

"Oh, is this Mr. Moony?"

"Yeah, sorry about that. I was expecting my wife."

"Oh, I see. This is Edwin Nelson. I decided to try you at this other number. I was afraid I'd get your wife."

Nelson's voice sounds shaky, and I don't think fear of Frankie accounts for all of it. I ask if he's okay, not that I really care.

"Yes, I'm all right, it's just been a very trying day. This little cat of yours is causing an awful lot of trouble."

"I don't think my cat's the one causing you trouble. I think it's you losing him that's causing the trouble."

"Well, yes, that's what I meant. Same difference."

I don't bother telling him it's not, though I sure am tempted. "I assume by now you had a chance to talk to Pat Ryan."

"Who?"

"Pat Ryan. He's a former police commander."

"Oh yes, of course, Mr. Ryan. Why are you mentioning him?"

"He's the one who referred me to you. Didn't he talk to you? He said he was going to stop by around noon hour."

"Oh no, I was gone then. I was at my club luncheon. We had ostrich today."

"Beg your pardon?"

"I'm in a club—we eat game."

"I see." That one stops me in my tracks. But I can't resist asking how it was.

He seems pleased that I do. "Rather disappointing, actually. The texture was a tad stringy, despite the fact that it was far more moist than I expected. It was greasier than goose, if you can imagine that. But the flavor lacked a certain richness in dimension that you customarily get with fowl. I like being an adventurer, but when it comes right down to it, I guess I'm just someone who's stuck on duck."

Now I get it. The guy is not only a crook, he's a quack.

"So anyway, I didn't have a chance to talk to Mr. Ryan. However, I did just now get off the phone with Mr. Ostrow."

"Oh, I'll bet that was great for your digestion."

"Well, yes, he was very upset. He seems to have the impression that I told you *he* might have stolen your cat."

"Dr. Nelson, Ron Ostrow is a sniveling, back-stabbing moron. And those are his good qualities. I didn't say anything to him that would even suggest you implicated him. And if he said I did, it's either because he's a liar or a bad listener or both."

"Well, yes, I mean, I didn't really think you would've said that I accused him. But Mr. Moony, you must understand, I can't have you driving away my customers."

"Dr. Nelson, I don't know how much business Ron Ostrow brings you, but if he's only one-tenth as big a pain in the ass as a customer as he was when he was my ambulance partner, then no amount would be enough."

"Well, actually, he doesn't pay me."

"What—you don't charge him?"

"Well, we have an arrangement."

"Yeah, and I'll bet he suggested it. It's called a shake-down."

"No, no, you're putting words in my mouth. He's a very high-ranking paramedic, and if—"

"What—if you get in a car accident, you just drop his name and they'll get you to the hospital faster? Give me a break." I'm usually nicer to people, but this guy is really trying my patience, especially after what Frankie learned about his credit history. "Let me tell you something, Edwin. I worked with Ron Ostrow. If you do get in some medical emergency and need an ambulance, you better pray he doesn't answer the call. Because if he does, your chances of ending up in the morgue will increase by a lot."

The sting of being humiliated by Ostrow is still fresh, so I'm exaggerating a bit. But I can say this: When I started working with him, Ostrow was carrying a pocket mirror to hold under a stiff's nose to help him figure out if a guy was still breathing.

"So, Dr. Nelson, let's stop talking about Ron Ostrow and start talking about my cat."

"Yes, yes, but Mr. Moony, I also hear that that you and your wife went out to my house this morning and barged in on my wife. Now that—"

I refrain from telling him that we didn't barge, because I suppose we did, though not in the sense that he means it. I doubt he's seen Rod putting Abby through her paces. "She had an ad in the newspaper, Doctor. We didn't know it was your wife until we got there. And by the way, that breeding business of hers. Is that a profitable venture? Looks to me like she's got some serious inventory problems."

"If you must know the truth, Mr. Moony, I'm about to shut down my wife's breeding operation, and she's none too pleased about it. But frankly, I don't think that's any of your damn business."

"You're right, it's not." I welcome Nelson's indignation. It makes me feel less like a bully. "But it is my business to wonder why you neglected to mention your wife's interest in cats when we talked yesterday. Especially considering her fascination with that particular breed."

"Yes, I understand, I know how that must look. But I'm sure you also understand that I didn't want to arouse your suspicions of her."

"Is that right? Well, guess what. You've managed to arouse my suspicions of both of you."

"Oh, come now, Mr. Moony. I'm a medical professional with a thriving practice. Do you really think I'd risk my reputation to steal a customer's cat? My entire operation would be on the line."

"You've been there before."

"Pardon me?"

"New Jersey, Ohio. I hear you have a stellar reputation in those states."

The silence lasts about half a minute before he manages to stammer out a reply. "What do you . . . But how did you—"

"My wife's a newspaper reporter. She did some checking on you. She had plenty of time to do it, while waiting for you to call her back, like you promised."

"I'm sorry about that—as I said, I was busy and preoccupied and—"

"And nervous? Yes, I imagine you were."

"Mr. Moony, I think you and I had better talk."

"We're talking now, Doctor."

"I mean *in* person, when I'm not facing a whole waiting room full of damn yappers!" His tone is somewhere between snippy and snappy. For a moment, I feel for the guy. It's the moment when he says that he's sorry and actually sounds like he means it. If I were in his shoes, I'd feel like I was about to snap too.

"We close at six tonight. How about if you come by around six-thirty I'll tell Madge to leave the door unlocked."

"That'd be fine. Will you have my cat there with you?"

"Mr. Moony, at this moment, I don't know where your cat is. But I do have an idea about who took him, and I think it will surprise you very much to hear it."

"Let's hear it. I love surprises."

"Not over the phone, not now. But I can tell you that I'm certain my wife does not have him, in case that's what you're thinking."

"And just how do you know that?"

"Because she told me, and I believe her. And besides that, I know her habits. She wouldn't be interested in your cat. She does not allow more than one stud at a time, and she already has that."

"You mean Bobo," I say, but I'm picturing Rod.

"Yes, that's right, Bobo. Now my wife does have some emotional problems. I'll admit that. And I'm sure you understand what it's like being married to someone like that."

I don't know if he means I should understand generally or specifically. "No, actually, I really don't, Doctor."

"Well, I mean, your wife."

That's what I thought he meant. "Dr. Nelson, my wife has a bad temper. She's not a kook. And she has ancestors from Sicily. Does that mean anything to you?"

"Mr. Moony, is that a threat? Because if it is, perhaps we should just turn this right over to the lawyers." He's still got some fight left in him, but when a guy's knockout punch involves going to his lawyer, it usually means he's got a glass jaw. "I know something about your background too, Mr. Moony. And I'm not sure it's so smart for me to be letting you come to my office."

"You want lawyers, Edwin? Fine. But the lawyers I'll turn it over to work for the state's attorney's office and the U.S. attorney's office and the IRS. Anyone I'm forgetting? The Department of the Interior, perhaps? Or maybe you'd like me to contact the membership director of the wild-game-eaters club?"

"Oh dear." His voice trails off, as if he's shrinking to the size of a toy poodle. When it comes back, it's filled with hollow optimism. "Mr. Moony, I'm afraid we've gotten off on the wrong foot. And I'm willing to start over, at square one, if you are."

"Sure, I'm willing to come talk to you, Doctor. But the way I see it, you're not at square one. You're right behind the eight ball. And if you want to get yourself in a better position, you'll need to come up with some answers."

Twelve

I'm feeling a bit smug after having the last word with Edwin Nelson. I'm one of those people who thrive on conflict—especially after a few midday beers—and there's simply been too damn little of it in my life lately. The pleasure of victory is a bit diluted by the stature of the opponent, but I remind myself that the stiff has stiffed quite a few folks and still lives high on the hog. Any guy who eats game is fair game in my book.

I don't have long to savor my conquest. A few moments later, Ma Bell provides another local caller to enliven my day.

"Hello, Mr. Moony." She doesn't identify herself and she knows she doesn't have to. I find it curious that the purr stays in Abby Nelson's voice long after the sleep has left her throat. Perhaps Rod is still there putting her through her morning paces.

"I hope I haven't gotten you into trouble with your wife."

"With my wife? Why would I be in trouble with my wife?"

"I just tried to call you at home but she answered. I disguised my voice so she wouldn't recognize me. But I don't think I completely fooled her."

"No, that's tough to do, she's pretty sharp."

"Yes, we girls have a word for that."

I don't inquire what that word might be, though I sense that she'd like me to. I just ask why she's calling.

"To apologize. You see, Mr. Moony, I understand how you're feeling. By the way, may I call you Phil?"

"Please do."

"Phil. Call me Abby. Please."

She seems to be waiting for it, so I oblige her. "Abby."

"There. Now we're friends." She lets out a little laugh. "As I was saying, I understand how hard it must be to have someone steal your cat. They're such beautiful luscious creatures. I think I know exactly how you're feeling." She shifts into the speech pattern that I thought was reserved only for Bobo. As she does, I picture her little bosom buddy catching twenty winks up in the balcony. "Phil, you mush be heartbroken."

"Yes, Abby, I am. But actually, I'm more angry than anything. I'm wondering what kind of person would do such a thing."

"I know, I know. There are some really terrible people out there. And that's one of the reasons I'm calling. Because I didn't want you to think I was one of them. Phil, I could never do such a thing."

"I see." This is clearly my moment to bring up her checkered past, but I have a feeling she may be taking her first step on a meandering path to a confession.

"I could never do something so terrible, Phil. It's important to me that you know that."

"It is?"

"Yes, of course. I understand the unique personal bond that some people develop with their cats. And I sense that you're one of those people, Phil. So I can feel your hurt."

"I see."

"Well, I can imagine it. Like Bobo and me. Phil, if I lost Bobo, I think I'd die. No, I'm sure I would."

She sounds like she means it. She also sounds like she had the same lunch I did, only without the patty melt and fries.

"Yes, I noticed that you two seem very close."

"Oh, we are. Close doesn't begin to describe it. Phil, we do everything together." At that moment, her voice gets farther away, and I realize she's sparing me the challenge of coming up with a response. "Yesh, that's right, we do, shweetie, don't we?" When she's back on with me, her voice is almost businesslike.

"So I'd like to help you any way I can. And I thought of something. I have several young male cats that I have to— I know this sounds terrible, but I have to get rid of them, and very soon."

"Why is that?"

"Why, Bobo—of course."

"I see. I guess he doesn't like having other male cats around."

"Are you kidding! He won't stand for it!" She breaks into Bobo-speak. "No you won't, shweetheart, will you? No no no no. Mama only needs one man around here, ishn't that right." She's back to me in sultry English. "So, Phil, you can have as many of my males as you want—for free."

"Abby, that's very generous of you, but—"

"Phil, I would have made the same offer this morning, but your wife was being such a . . . well, she was being very sharp, shall we say?"

"Oh yeah, her claws were definitely showing a bit. And that's very nice of you to offer, but I couldn't do that."

"Why not?"

The real reason is that I'd rather have a nuclear power plant in my backyard than a new cat in my house, but I'm sure that's not something she'd understand.

"Abby," I say, "I don't think my cat and I have nearly as intimate a relationship as you and Bobo do, but I do feel a very special attachment to him. You see, he belonged to my father. After my father died, I took him in."

"Oh, I hated my father."

Some lines even I know better than to touch. "In any event, I don't think any other cat could substitute for Phull."

"Who?"

"That's the name of my cat—Phull."

"Phil and Phull. How darling."

I'm tempted to tell her about the history of the name, but I give her the short version. "That's not his original name. His original name was Edwin, like your husband."

"You're kidding. Someone changed his name? Who—your wife?"

"No. My father."

"That's the kind of thing a father would do—change the poor cat's name. It's no wonder he was urinating all over your house. He was trying to reclaim the territory of his name."

"Gosh, do you really think so?"

"I know so. It's obvious. You don't change a cat's name. It's part of their identity. That's a very cruel thing to do."

"I see. So when I find him—if I find him—do you suggest I start calling him Edwin again?"

"Phil." She sighs. "That's a very tough call. I'm glad I'm not in your situation. But if you'd be willing to let me spend some time with him, I think I could advise you on what to do."

"Certainly. But first, I have to find him."

"I don't think that should be too hard."

"You don't?"

"No, all you have to do is track down the man who picked him up yesterday."

There are days when I wonder if it's me or the rest of the world. Talking to Abby Nelson, I realize it's the rest of the world, though she does appear to have a world of her very own.

84

"Abby, that's what I've been trying to find out."

"It was a cop."

"Beg your pardon?"

"The man who picked up Phull—I mean Edwin—he was a cop."

"How do you know that?"

"I saw his badge."

"He was wearing a badge?"

"No, not wearing it. It was on his wallet. I saw it when he went to pay me."

"Abby, this morning you said you couldn't remember who picked Phull up."

"Yes I know, but I just said that. Phil, I was overwrought, and your wife was being . . . sharp, remember? I just didn't feel like telling her anything. But you, Phil, you're a whole different breed. I'd tell you anything."

I wonder if that's what she's doing right now, or whether there's actually some truth to what she's saying. "Then tell me what he looked like."

"He was in his forties, average height, well-built and Irish."

"How do you know he was Irish?"

"Reddish hair, pug nose, freckles, bloodshot eyes. That would be Irish, wouldn't you say?"

"Most of the time, yes. Tell me about the badge. Are you sure it was a police badge?"

"What other kind is there?"

I don't see any point in explaining how every bozo who gets paid seven bucks an hour to sit in a bank lobby gets to wear a badge. The thing I'm wondering about is if it was someone on the fire department.

"Was it a star?" I ask. "Or was it a shield?"

"I don't know—a star, I guess." That means it was a cop.

"Was it silver or gold?" This has to do with rank.

"Gold, I think it was gold. No, I'm wrong, it was silver. It's the other cop that came in, he has the gold one."

85

"What other cop?"

"Mr. Ryan."

"Patrick Ryan?"

"Yes, I think so, I don't know. I just know him as Mr. Ryan. He's retired, I think."

Assuming she's talking about my pal, she's got the color of the badge right. Pat had a rank of commander, and anyone above lieutenant gets gold. But I suspect she's confused about when he was at the office.

"When you saw Mr. Ryan, are you talking about today, or yesterday?"

"I wasn't there today. I only work on Friday. I do the files and assist Edwin with surgery."

"But yesterday was a Monday, and you were there then."

"I know, I had to fill in for the regular receptionist. She was getting her toes done or something. She always picks the most inconvenient times to be out. I had to miss my workout and I felt terrible all day."

"Mr. Ryan had his cats there yesterday also?"

"No, he was just buying food. He does that for some reason."

"I see. And the man with my cat, the Irish-looking guy—you're sure he had a silver star. It wasn't a shield?"

"I don't understand—what's the difference?"

"If it's a silver shield, that means he might have worked for the fire department."

"Oh, I don't know. Phil, it was busy. I think it was a star, but I can't be positive. I'm sorry."

"No, don't be, that's okay. You're being very helpful. Now, have you ever seen this man before? Is he one of your regular customers?"

"No, of course not." She lets out a throaty laugh. "Phil, are you taking stupid pills, or what? If he was one of our regular customers, then I'd know his name, right?"

"Yes, I suppose you would." Unless it was a customer who

doesn't come in on Friday, when she works, or Monday, when Madge likes to have her toes done. "Was there anything that seemed strange about the guy?"

"Well, yes, now that you mention it. He didn't seem to have any rapport with the cat. He didn't speak to him or pet him, he just wanted me to put him right in his cat box. And when I told him what a wonderful breed of cat it was, he didn't seem all that interested. When I told him Edwin wasn't able to find anything wrong, he didn't ask any questions. Of course, if I had known about this terrible name-change business, I would have been able to tell him a whole lot more. Phil, I truly believe that the name change is the root cause of his problems. When you find him, call me. I'm sure I can help. Edwin is a good vet in the medical sense, but he doesn't understand the psychological dimension. So please come see me."

"Thank you, I will."

"Without your wife, if you don't mind. Nothing personal against her, but I think that would be better, if you know what I mean."

"I think I do, but I also think that you two maybe just got off on the wrong paw."

She laughs. "Phil, I'd love to talk to you longer, but I have to start thinking about dinner. If it's not on the table the moment he gets home, Edwin is grouchy as a bear."

"I think he already had bear for lunch."

"Pardon? Oh, that's right. It's game-club Tuesday. Then all I'll need is the Tums."

"Maybe I should bring them. I'm going to see him at the office at six-thirty."

"You're meeting with Edwin? Why?"

"We just have to talk about a few things."

"He didn't say a word to me about it."

"I only spoke to him a little while ago. It was too busy at the office to talk on the phone. He suggested that I come."

Her voice changes from sulky back to sultry. "Phil, you're not planning on suing us, are you? We can't afford another lawsuit."

I don't see any point in telling her it's one of my options. "I'm just trying to get my cat back. I'm not planning on suing anyone."

"Thank you, Phil. I'm so glad it's you and not one of our other customers. If I can be of any help, please don't hesitate to call me. I mean it. I do understand your pain."

"Thank you."

"It's nothing, really. Well, good-bye, Phil. The Tums should be extra-strength, tropical flavor. Edwin is a very finicky eater."

Thirteen

By the time I hang up with Abby Nelson, I've got a serious case of phone ear. So when the damn thing rings a few moments later, I'm tempted to ignore it.

I know it's Frankie, eager to find out just what the wacky cat lady had to say for herself and just as eager to pierce my ear about my critical need to get call-waiting. That way, she could have had the privilege of interrupting our conversation instead of being rebuffed by a busy signal.

But I can't ignore my wife. Never have, never will.

It's Pat Ryan. "Well, it looks like our Dr. Nelson is looking to become the go-to guy for coppers." When Pat's in his work mode, he dispenses with pleasantries and cuts right to the chase.

"There's four that I recognize right away from his customer list. He's got quite a niche for himself."

"Maybe more like an itch."

"Come again?"

"An *itch*. I think he likes sucking up to people he perceives as powerful." I tell him about Nelson's payment arrangement with Ron Ostrow.

"Oh, and what fine powers of perception about the powerful he seems to have. I thought he was silly enough making that offer to me, a retired cop. But trying to buy influence with a paramedic! The guy's a bigger stiff than I thought."

"I thought he came with your highest recommendation."

"No, I never said that. I just said he seems like a good vet. I didn't say I wanted to go out to dinner with him."

"You definitely wouldn't want to go to lunch with him."

"Why do you say that?"

I tell him about Nelson's idea of lean cuisine. That provokes a rare howl. It's easy to get a rise out of Pat, but, like most cops, the kind of rise you get is about the same as from baking bread. Most of the yeast comes right out of him when I begin to relate our morning visit with Abby Nelson.

"Hey, I thought you agreed to let me handle this. You were going to avoid doing anything crazy, remember?"

"I know, I know. But Frankie was dead-set on going." When in trouble, blame your spouse. That's one of the overlooked benefits of being married. "Do you think you would have been able to stop her?"

Pat gives the only answer he can—a long, defeated sigh. "Okay, go on. Tell me what happened."

I start in giving him the whole blow-by-blow—from Rod to Bobo. He stops me when I get to Frankie and Abby's knock-down-drag-out.

"Oh, I knew there had to be a cat fight coming. Madge says Abby is a real witch."

"And Abby had nothing but kind words for Madge when she called me this afternoon."

"She called you back? What did she say about Madge?"

"Just a few pointed references. If you put the three of them in a room with one scratching post, you'd have quite a rumble."

Pat chuckles. "I think I'd pay to see that."

"Frankie would win, paws down."

"I don't know. Madge can be pretty tenacious."

"Maybe in her prime, Pat. But with those bunions, she can't be too quick on her feet."

"You know about her bunions?"

"Don't underestimate my skills as an investigator." I tell him about the skeletons from Ohio and New Jersey that Nelson has hiding in his closet.

"Very impressive. And how'd you manage to find all that out?"

"My wife told me."

"That's real fast—even for her."

"Computers, Pat. They're changing our lives."

"I've got one. All I can do is play solitaire and make greeting cards."

"You've never sent one to me."

"Yeah, I know. I can't figure out how to make the damn thing print."

"Don't feel bad, it's the thought that counts."

I fill Pat in on my phone calls with Nelson and his wife. He thinks I may have come down too hard on the little vet and too easy on his little pet. Nelson, he says, is in the difficult position of having to cover for her, and according to Madge, Abby is every bit as devious as she is crazy. He's also skeptical about her story that a cop picked up Phull, if only because a cop should have been smart enough to keep his badge out of sight.

"I've heard lots of stories about dumb cops, Pat. Quite a few of them from you."

"Yeah, this is true. And sometimes it's more a matter of arrogance than lack of intelligence."

"But I'm inclined to think she was mistaken about the badge. I think it was probably a shield."

"I see. One of your old buddies from the fire department."

"One of Ron Ostrow's buddies from the fire department. He was there when Frankie dropped Phull off. He easily could have overheard when she was planning to pick him up."

"That's plausible. You'll need to have a look at the customer list—see if there's anyone you recognize. But for now I think the cat lady is our number-one suspect."

"Nelson sounded convinced that she didn't take him."

"I'm sure he'd like to believe that. He may change his story after we talk to him."

"Great; you'll come with me?"

"I'll meet you there. On two conditions."

"And they are?"

"One, you let me do the talking. If this guy's as nervous about the law as he ought to be, I can make a lot better headway than you."

"Sure. And two?"

"Be on time for a change."

That one I know better than to make any promises about. I have an aversion to punctuality that dates back to my mother's insistence that we get to mass at least fifteen minutes early. But I do agree to try my best.

"Phil, you'll need to do better than that."

As soon as Pat hangs up, I do the dutiful thing and call my dear wife.

"What's going on? I've been trying to reach you for—"

"I know, I'm sorry. And I really should get call-waiting."

"That goes without saying. What I want to know is what dear Abby had to say that kept you on the phone for a whole hour. Did she confess to catnapping or was she just giving advice? Or maybe she just wanted to purr in your ear?"

"No confession. Just an apology for being so rude this morning and an offer to replace Phull with as many male cats as you could wish for—free of charge."

"That sounds an awful lot like a confession to me."

"I don't think so. And just for the record, I was on with Pat after she called, so I didn't spend the whole hour talking with her."

"You called Pat before you reported in to me? Where do your loyalties lie?"

"*He* called *me*."

"No way. I was hitting redial every two minutes."

"I guess his timing's better than yours."

"And yours couldn't be worse. I'm on my way out the door."

"Where are you going?"

"I'm having a drink with Charlotte, remember?" Charlotte Penske is a gossip columnist for the *Sun-Times*. She's also one of Chicago's most celebrated lushes.

"A drink? Isn't that an oxymoron?"

"No, it's the inverse of hyperbole. Maybe we'll splurge and have two. And we'll probably have a little dinner."

"*Two* drinks?"

"Stop that. Did Abby have anything useful to say?"

"Maybe. She thinks the guy who picked up Phull was a cop."

"Really? This morning she said she didn't remember who picked him up."

"She said she just said that because you were being so rude to her."

"I see. And what about you?"

"Apparently, I came off like a perfect gentleman. And someone with a rare sensitivity to cats."

"A rare breed indeed. What's this about the guy being a cop?"

"I'm thinking it might be fire department. She says the guy had a badge in his wallet—she didn't notice if it was a star or a shield."

"Oh yes, they look so much alike."

"To someone with her head in the clouds, they might."

"I think her head's buried in the litter box. And I've got to scoot."

"Just one more thing. I thought you'd like to know that the other half of the dynamic Nelson duo finally called back."

"And what did the dear doctor have to say? Did you ask about his habit of losing cats?"

"Yes, I did. He stammered a lot and said his wife has some emotional problems."

"Well, isn't he a perceptive sort! Did you learn anything interesting?"

"He's a member of a game-eaters club. Does that count?"

"Oh, Jesus. You mean he's one of those tired old bores who sit around that silly lodge on Grand Avenue eating boar?"

"I didn't even know there was such a place. I just know that they had ostrich for lunch today."

"Oh, how delicious. What a creep. Oh dear!"

"What's the matter?"

"You don't think Nelson snatched Phull, do you?"

"What—you mean to eat him? Frankie, I don't think it was a potluck. And if it was, I think he could've had the pick of the litter right back at his house."

"Of course, you're right. I'm sorry. My head's already down at the bar. And Charlotte's will be on the bar. I've really got to go."

"Okay, but here's one more thing to think about."

"Make it quick, please, darling."

"If the vet did eat our cat for lunch, that would make him a Phull Nelson."

"Uh-huh. I think that was my line."

"Isn't plagiarism the sincerest form of flattery to a writer?"

"That depends on who collects the royalties. In this case there aren't any—so I'm flattered. Don't bother waiting up for me."

"I'll leave the light on and the aspirin out."

Fourteen

I miss the action. I miss lots of things about my old job, but mostly I miss the action. When you ride on an ambulance, you rule the streets. You go where few people are permitted, and you do it with impunity and purpose. Traffic parts for you like the Red Sea did for Moses, pedestrians obediently make room for you on crowded sidewalks. Hell, even the cops get out of your way when you're working on an accident scene. There's definitely a power trip to it, and that's certainly what some paramedics get off on. But the guys who are in it for the power are the ones who didn't make it onto the cops. If you want power, become a cop. If you want action, join the fire department.

Expecting the unexpected has a lot to do with it. You start each shift not knowing where you'll be going. But you know that wherever you end up going, most people will be curious to know what's going on there. Emergencies attract everyone's attention. There can be close calls, bogus calls, and calls that come too late. On one level, they bring a dose of instant drama to otherwise ordinary life. On another, they provide an opportunity to get close to life's greatest mystery, death. Being the guy people call on in an emergency gives you a free pass to the action. The moment that call comes in, you become part of the action.

It's not all saving lives. Most of the time it's not about saving lives. Lots of times it's just providing an escort service for people who are too poor or too lazy or too stupid to get themselves to a doctor. As many people as you find bleeding at car accidents, you find just as many at home sitting in front of their TVs. Sometimes it can be dull. But even when it's dull, there are stories to tell.

I once had back-to-back calls that should have been directed to a plumber. They both involved the obese. One guy had become so comfortably engrossed in the latest issue of *Hustler* that he'd managed to get his butt wedged into the seat of his commode. We handled that one with a screwdriver, a pry-bar and an assist from gravity. Two hours later, we were called to another bathroom, where a woman of remarkable girth had become so comfortably engrossed in a Danielle Steele novel that her back had gotten stuck against the wall of her bathtub like a suction cup. All that one took was a little "slide of hand." Abracadabra, right down her spine, and she popped free like the cork on a bottle of wine.

Sometimes, of course, it is about saving lives, and when your efforts make the difference between someone living and someone dying, the satisfaction is immense. Those are the heroic moments, the ones that some paramedics live for. I wasn't one of those, because I figured that luck plays as big a role in heroics as the hero does. For every moment of heroic satisfaction, there's inevitably another one that isn't so satisfying—from the teenage girl who got into the wrong car with the wrong boy to the infant who simply stopped breathing. You lose a life and you wonder what you could have done better; if you could have done better. The what-ifs can haunt you if you let them. If you're the sort of person who lets them, you should look for another line of work.

I didn't let the what-ifs bother me. I didn't let the heroic moments go to my head. I didn't get off on the power trip. I saw it all as action, and that's what I miss.

This situation with Dr. Edwin Nelson is the most action I've had for a long time. Which is a rather sad commentary on one part of my life. As I get into my car, I can feel my heart beating a little faster than usual. I'm ready to turn on the siren and race to the scene. But the fact is, I've got some time to kill.

I always seem to have time to kill. And if I don't get used to that, it's going to be the death of me.

I stop at a little tavern on Milwaukee Avenue for a couple of pops. That should calm me down a bit. The TV news is on, and it's business as usual. Two more aldermen have been indicted on corruption charges. The lawyers for both of them say that their clients were entrapped. At a press conference Mayor Dickie reminds everyone that a man is innocent beyond a shadow of a doubt until proved guilty. Everything will be fine, he says, as soon as the City Council passes his sweeping new ethics ordinance. When the City Hall reporter for the *Tribune* asks why the ethics ordinance doesn't prohibit him from handing out no-bid contracts to his largest campaign contributors, the Mayor goes into his fish-eye glare: "Why in the world would we ever want to do that for?"

Ethics Chicago style, I'll drink to that. Damn, I love this city. When I step back out into the early evening air, I can feel the approaching chill of winter peeking out from beneath the worn-out blanket of October warmth. I also realize that the beers have had an unintended effect: I'm loaded for bear. I have to remind myself that the prey I'm stalking is an owl-eyed little man who ate ostrich for lunch.

There's a parking space in the lot right outside Purr & Bark, but I still opt for a spot on the street. Just my little rebellion against the city, being turned into a strip mall. As I get out of my car and start across the parking lot, it occurs to me that the circumstance I'm about to enter is a highly charged situation. Edwin Nelson may be a little guy, but he does have a lot at stake. I'm glad that Pat agreed to come with me. And I'm pleased with myself for arriving two minutes early. I decide to wait for him before going in.

I give it five minutes before giving the door a go. It sticks and I have to give it the shoulder treatment. Pat may already be inside.

Behind the door, I feel two senses engage strongly. The odor of pets hangs heavy in the air, and the aroma of air freshener hangs even heavier. The place is eerily silent, with me accounting for the only sound.

Someone has drawn the drapes and shut out most of the lights. I call out Nelson's name through the dim fluorescence. Three times, each one a bit louder. On the fourth, I shout it out and add Pat's name to the monologue.

Even though Nelson is expecting me, I feel like an intruder as I go behind the reception desk to the door to the backroom. I open that and call his name again. Three more times, and Pat's too. I'm still the only producer of sound in the place. I pause and consider going back outside to wait for Pat. I remind myself that curiosity killed the cat.

But not all cats. I move into the hallway area where Nelson and Madge and I had our little powwow yesterday and finally hear evidence of another being. It's a scratching noise coming from around the corner to the left. I call the vet's name again as I move toward there. At the corner, the hall gives way to an open room. When I get there, I can identify the source of the scratching sound.

It's a chorus of sounds, actually, coming from cats perched in wooden cages mounted to the wall. There are half a dozen cats, a dozen cages. The cages are painted in pastels, the only spark of color in the room. The rest of it is a sea of gray. None of the cats is mine. There are three large steel cages on the floor. One of them is occupied by a dog, a golden retriever. At first I wonder why he didn't bark, but when he opens his sleepy eyes to look at me, I can see that he's in his golden years and his barking days are mostly behind him. But it's no wonder why Dr. Edwin Nelson didn't answer me when I barked. It's hard to speak when your mouth is kissing the floor. When your mouth is kissing the floor, that usually means your heart isn't in it. When your heart's no longer in it, it's impossible to say anything at all.

My first thought is that it must have been something he ate. I remember that I forgot the Tums. But I don't forget what I have to do. Once you're trained, you never forget. It's like riding a bicycle.

In this case, the bicycle has two flat tires and a broken chain. I can tell as soon as I roll him over that Edwin Nelson isn't likely to be riding anywhere under his own power. His eyelids are closed, but that just means they got a little help from gravity on the way down to the floor. I can see it was a hard fall, because his nose and mouth are bloodied from the impact and he left a couple of teeth on the linoleum tile. But there's not a lot of blood, which means his heart probably stopped pumping before he toppled over.

It's the good doctor's pallor that's the dead giveaway. He's dusky gray, and he'd blend in perfectly with the bland decor of the room if it weren't for the white lab coat providing a bit of contrast. But old habits die hard, so I get right to work, even though I know it's a lost cause.

I check for a pulse at his wrist. Nothing doing there. Then I try the carotid artery. Nothing there either. I move my hands to his mouth to open his airway, but the blood gives me pause.

In the old days, there wouldn't have been any hesitation. But that was before we all learned about AIDS. These days an EMT isn't allowed to lay a hand on anyone before putting on surgical gloves. I think that's an overreaction, but when it comes to the possibility of contracting AIDS, I guess paranoia has come to be seen as the better part of caution.

You can make the case that a victim's likelihood of having AIDS should be a factor in whether you waste precious time to protect yourself first. But if you're going to worry about contracting AIDS at all, you can make just as strong a case that you can never be sure about anyone. For a while, I taught emergency medicine classes, and I'd present the following scenario to my students:

You're called to the home of a widow in her seventies who appears to have suffered a heart attack. This is a classic case of someone who is not at risk for AIDS. She's not likely to be an intravenous drug user and she probably hasn't had multiple sex partners. But what if she had been hospitalized for a gall-bladder operation three years before and she had received a blood transfusion? What if the blood was tainted? It's about as likely a scenario as winning the lottery twice in the same week, but is it a chance you'd be willing to take? I know plenty of people who buy lottery tickets, though I'm not one of them.

In the case of Dr. Nelson, two things give me good reason to resort to precautions. One, there's the blood, right out there, just waiting for contact. Two, there are his chances for survival, which appear to depend more on divine intervention rather than the efforts of a mere mortal like me. But I'm the closest thing to a supreme being that Nelson has going for him right now, so it's my responsibility not to give up just yet.

I'm sure the guy has a supply of surgical gloves somewhere in the office, but I don't need to search through cabinets or drawers. As luck would have it, Nelson is wearing a pair. And I don't think he'd mind if I borrow them.

As I grab his right hand to strip one off, I find reason to wonder if there's any luck here for me after all. The hand is clenched into a tight fist, which is odd considering Nelson's present condition. As I pry open the hand to begin tugging on the glove, my fingers come into contact with an object that the hand has been clutching.

It's a small cylindrical object, so when I knock it loose from Nelson's hand, it rolls about three linoleum tiles from his body before coming to a stop. That's not even half as far away as it would have landed if Nelson had been holding it before he fell. The sight of it makes me stop and shudder.

It's a hypodermic syringe. And if I'm not mistaken, it now has my fingerprints on it. That thought makes me shudder some more. It's one of about five hundred thoughts that rise to the surface of my beer-dampened brain all at once. Talk about your head swimming; mine's about to drown.

I try to focus on what I should do next, but the options are too numerous and all of them seem undesirable. I tell myself the fingerprints shouldn't be a problem. I can always wipe them off. I think about doing that right away. But I should talk to Pat first, see what he thinks. Where the hell is Pat anyway? Why did I pick this occasion to be on time for once? And why did he pick it to be late for the first time ever?

There's one way the fingerprints definitely won't be a problem—if I can manage to raise Edwin Nelson from the dead. I decide to return to that hopeless task and let Pat handle the questions that the cops are sure to ask.

I strip Nelson's gloves off and put them on. I wipe away all the blood I can from his mouth, then press down the back of his tongue to clear the airway at the oral pharynx. I put my mouth near his and give him two quick breaths. In return for my efforts, I get the unmistakable whiff of corpse breath. That's a very foul odor that ranks somewhere between the breath of a dog and a drunken menthol-cigarette smoker. I check the carotid for a pulse anyway and naturally get nothing. I stack the palms of my hands together and start in on the chest compressions.

"Start breathing, you goddamn little wimp," I hear myself say. Then I hear Pat's voice, and I practically jump out of my skin. I'd be startled by any sound now, but the added surprise is that he enters from the back of the office rather than from the way I came in.

"What the hell's going on?" he asks. "Did he have a heart attack?"

"Yeah—and you almost gave me one." I take a break from pressing on Nelson's chest to clutch mine for a moment.

"Sorry about that. What happened?"

"It looks like our vet's been euthanized."

I follow Pat's gaze until it stops on the syringe. "What—you mean he killed himself?"

I give Nelson two more futile breaths, then shake my head. "No. I don't think so. I think someone wanted it to look that way."

"What makes you think that?"

I begin thumping on Nelson's chest again. I'm short of breath when I answer Pat's question. "He hit the floor like a ton of bricks—face first. But the syringe stays in his hand, with his fist clenched tight around it. It should've flown across the room when he fell; it might have broken, too."

"Yeah, probably. So how'd it get where it is now?"

"That's the problem. I pulled it out of his hand when I was trying to get off his surgical glove."

"You mean you touched it."

"Yup." I turn back to Nelson.

"And why'd you do a dumb thing like that?"

"I didn't see it. It was hidden in his hand."

Pat lets out a long sigh.

"Is that a big problem?"

He nods. "Could be." He pulls his handkerchief out of his pocket, walks to the syringe and picks it up. He wipes the syringe with the cloth, then holds it lightly through the handkerchief. "Where exactly did you find him?"

I take a break from Nelson's chest and motion with my hand. "Facedown right on the teeth." There are three of them, probably not real teeth, but a bridge of fakes.

Pat nods, takes two steps back to where Nelson might have been standing, leans forward and lets the syringe drop.

It bounces and kicks to the right before rolling to near the base of the giant cat cabinet.

"Now it's not a problem," he says.

"Excuse me, officer, but isn't that called tampering with evidence?"

If he's the slightest bit amused, he's not letting on. "No, it's not. What you did is called tampering with evidence. *That* is called saving your pal's dumb ass." He gestures toward Nelson. "Does he have a shot in hell of making it?"

"None whatsoever. But I'd rather not be the one to make that call."

"Don't worry. I wouldn't let you be." Pat turns and heads toward the front room. "I'm phoning for medics and coppers. I'm calling it in as a probable suicide. Which it still might be, by the way, though I doubt it. So when the coppers get here, don't go advancing any homicide theories, okay, Phil? Let me do the talking."

"That's fine with me, boss. I wouldn't have it any other way."

As I start back in on Nelson, I speak to myself. "You said you wanted action? Well now, you've got it."

Fifteen

ow's the old doc doing?" Pat asks when he returns to the backroom.

"Even deader than he was two minutes ago, I'm afraid."

"Well, there goes my free veterinary services."

"Free? Do you mean to say you took Nelson up on his offer?"

"Sure, why not?"

"You're the squeaky-clean guy who always refused to take even a cup of coffee."

"That's when I was a copper. Now I'm just a lonely old pensioner."

"Gentlemen, start your violins. Do you think—"

"POLICE! Is anybody back there?" The voice comes like the sound of a large dog barking from the waiting room. It's immediately followed by a distinctly female tone, one that brings to mind a small mutt, coming from the back. "PO-LICE."

"Jesus, that's the fastest response time on record," Pat says. Then he raises his voice to pit-bull level. "Here, in the back-room. I'm a cop. And there's a dying man here."

Pat tells me to stay down working on Nelson. He waits

for the cops with one hand raised, holding his wallet open to show his badge.

The uniforms converge on the room at the same time. I glance up to see a tall thin redhead and a short dumpy brown-haired one. The redhead is the male model and the one who takes charge.

"What's going on here?"

"I'm Pat Ryan, former deputy commander. That's Edwin Nelson, the vet who owns this place."

"Yes, sir, I recognize your name. I'm Mike O'Malley, this is Officer Strayhorn. We're responding to a report of a prowler. Have you seen anyone?"

"No, just us. This is Phil Moony, he's an EMT."

I nod but don't look up.

"How's he doing?" Strayhorn asks me.

"Lousy, real lousy."

"Shirley, call an ambulance."

"I already did that, Mike," Pat says. "I called for coppers too."

"What happened? Did he have a heart attack?"

Pat points to the syringe. "It looks like he committed suicide."

Strayhorn takes a step toward the cat cage to have a closer look.

"Don't touch that, Shirley. It could be evidence."

"I wasn't about to touch it, Mike. I was just looking."

O'Malley speaks to Pat. "Did you know Mr. Whats-his-name?"

"Dr. Nelson. Yes, he was my vet."

"Was he having any personal problems, or was he depressed about anything, do you know?"

"I didn't know him that well." Pat shrugs. "If he killed himself, I'd guess he was probably depressed."

"How long have you two been here?"

"About fifteen minutes. We got here around six-thirty."

"Was the vet's office still open then?" Shirley asks.

"No, he left the door open for us."

"Why—were you picking up a pet?"

Pat nods. "We came to talk to him about Phil's cat."

Strayhorn speaks to O'Malley. "I'm going to go talk to the clerk."

"Yeah, good idea. And get us a cup of coffee while you're there."

She shoots him a look as she goes by, but he doesn't appear to notice. I do, and I'm still busy giving Nelson his second-to-last rites.

"A clerk at the White Hen's the one that called in the report," O'Malley says. "I have a hunch she probably saw one of you two."

A moment later, O'Malley looks like a guy who's good with his hunches. Shirley isn't holding any coffee, but she's got her hands full guiding the shoulders of a woman who's old enough to be her mother and big enough to be her sister.

"This is Mrs. Pleasance," she says. "She was waiting right outside." She makes a sweeping motion to take in Pat and me and Nelson. "Is one of these men the man you saw, Edith?"

"Oh yes, he's the one, definitely him." Edith's finger is pointing at me, but her eyes are on the fallen vet. "What about Edwin?" she asks. "Is he dead?"

It strikes me as odd that Edith is on a first-name basis with Dr. Nelson. "I'm doing all I can," I say.

"Such a nice man." She shakes her head sadly. "He comes in for tea and Tums every afternoon."

I nod. "Tropical flavor."

"What's that horrible smell?"

I'm a little surprised that she's the first one to mention it. "Dr. Nelson had a little accident," I say. "It happens some-times when people have heart attacks."

"Oh, of course, I should know that. I used to be a nurse." Edith looks as if her eyes wouldn't mind staying but her nose isn't sure she can. Maybe that's why she gave up nursing for a career at White Hen. O'Malley helps her decide by taking up shoulder duty and turning her toward the front room.

"Would you like some coffee, officer?"

"That's a fine idea, Mrs. Pleasance."

Shirley turns to Pat. "I thought you said you both got here together, at the same time."

Pat shakes his head. "No, I didn't. I said we both got here around six-thirty."

"He's right, Shirley, I was listening to him."

"Phil came in the front way, I came in the back."

"Why did you come in the back?"

"I usually do, when I'm picking up a pet after hours. Dr. Nelson leaves the back door open for me."

"Well, if you didn't get here together, which one of you got here first?"

"I did." Pat's answer surprises me. Enough so that I look up at him. He avoids my glance. "And now, Miss Strayhorn, if you're through with this line of questioning, I'd like to take a moment to advise you on something. The next time you have a possible witness and a possible suspect—which you don't in this case—try to avoid introducing them. If you end up charging the suspect, that can have a very unfortunate effect on the witness list at the trial, if you get my drift."

Shirley nods. "I think it might be a good idea if we open a window in here."

Before she can figure out the crank handle, a bit of fresh air arrives in a different form, a blast from my past.

"Whoa, baby, what did this guy have for lunch?" Van McNulty has added four inches of waist and lost two inches of hair since I last saw him. Which wasn't so long ago, at a funeral of a mutual friend who had put on eight inches of waist and lost ninety percent of his circulation.

I don't tell McNulty about the ostrich, because he's already on to his second and third questions.

"Moony! What the hell are you doing here? Is this guy a friend of yours?"

"No, I'm on Good Samaritan duty." I show him my bloody glove, as an excuse for not shaking hands.

"Oh, that's right, you don't have any friends." He's unloading his gear from his bag as he talks. "Okay, Phil, what've you got for me?"

"Triple zero." That's paramedic lingo for no pulse, no respiration, no blood pressure. Which translates, ninety-nine percent of the time, to *no chance*. "There's a hypodermic over there on the floor. I think he poked himself."

McNulty lays out a sheet, and I help him and his partner move Nelson onto it. As we do, two more cops arrive, another male-and-female tandem.

"Phil, this is my new partner, Jason Green. Jason, meet the infamous Phil Moony."

"Hi, I've heard a lot about you."

"You have?"

"Yeah, Moony, they're still talking about you. That's how dull things have gotten." McNulty puts on his gloves. "You two guys have something in common. You both went to Boyola." The reference is to my high school alma mater, Loyola Academy. "Only by the time Jason got there, they were already letting girls in."

"Imagine that." Officer Strayhorn is looking a little better since opening the window. "Pretty soon they'll be letting girls on the fire department."

"You went there too," I remind him.

"Yeah, but you two graduated." McNulty hands me the intravenous tube. "You can start a line on him if you want, Phil."

I look to Jason to see if that's okay with him.

"As I told you, Jason's my new partner, Phil. Why don't you start the line?"

Gotcha. This is McNulty's way of saying that young Jason could use some more training.

"Watch what he does, Jason. I'll start bagging him." McNulty takes the endotracheal tube and moves up by Nelson's head. You put that in an unconscious person's mouth to keep the airway open at the oral pharynx, where the tongue meets the throat. There's a plastic bag on the end of it about the size of a football. When you start CPR on someone, the bag provides a regular flow of air.

I take the syringe and grip Nelson's left arm. I have to tie off above the elbow to get a good shot at the antecubital vein on the soft side of his elbow. To do that, I have to roll up the sleeve of his lab coat a little more. I don't say anything, but I see marks on the arm, five small reddish impressions. Someone's hand was squeezing it not so long ago. I shoot a glance at Jason to see if he's noticed, but his face is drawing a blank. I glance back at the cops, but they don't seem to notice, either.

On the inside of Nelson's elbow, I see a tiny blood smear, which marks the injection site where someone has already popped him. It's dead on the vein, an indication that whoever administered the shot knew exactly what he was doing. My effort is dead-on too, but it won't be nearly as successful in meeting its objective. It would take a lot more than saline to counter the effects of what was injected previously. Epinephrine might have helped, but it's way too late for that now.

As I inject the needle, the blood that backs up into the hypodermic tube is pitch-black. I glance at Jason as he stares at the blood. "It's all over but the paperwork, kid."

"Yeah, thanks a bunch, Moony," McNulty says. "Jason, you can go get the stretcher. It's time to go get this guy pronounced."

"Which hospital are you taking him to?" Strayhorn asks.

"Resurrection. Not that there's any chance of that."

"Does anyone know if he's got family?"

"I think just a wife," I say. "They live on Hill Road in Winnetka."

Strayhorn looks at O'Malley. "Do you want to call?"

"No, you do it. I think it needs a lady's touch."

"Oh, brother."

McNulty shakes his head. "How long ago did you find this guy, Moony—yesterday?"

Just then I notice a clock on the wall across from the cat cage. It's hard not to notice, because it's announcing the hour with a series of high-pitched barks. I'll bet the cats just love that.

"Half an hour at most," I say. "He couldn't have been out much longer than that, because the place closes at six."

"Any idea what he shot himself with?"

With the marks on Nelson's arm offering more evidence than the syringe I touched, I'm tempted to mention my doubts about Nelson doing himself in. But I decide to follow Pat's instructions.

"Sodium pentobarbital. I'd bet the farm on it."

McNulty nods. "There's probably enough of it around here."

"What's that?" asks O'Malley.

"They use it to put dogs to sleep," I say.

"And how do you know that?"

"We're EMTs. We know a little something about drugs. And also—"

"And also," booms another voice entering the room, "if you're an EMT named Philip Moony, you know a whole lot about drugs. Isn't that right, Mr. Moony?"

I wheel around to match the voice with a face. It's not a face that I recognize, but from now on, it's one that I won't forget. The guy's mouth takes up more than half of it, leaving room for only a very small nose and eyes with reclining sockets. The nose may be only for decoration, since the guy is using the mouth to breathe.

"And also"—I look back at O'Malley and repeat the sentence I started—"I read the label on the syringe over there."

I look up at the cop with the big mouth. "I don't believe I've had the pleasure."

"Believe me, Phil," Pat says, "it's no pleasure."

"You're a stitch, Patrick." The guy lets out a laugh as he flashes his badge. "Dick Slopitch, Violent Crimes."

"Violent Crimes?" It's the male half of the second pair of cops who came in. "I'm Officer Callaway. Someone called you here?"

"I was in the neighborhood. I like to listen to the radio. I hear a report of a prowler, then a possible suicide called in by a former high-ranking member of the department. It sounds like something worth checking out. So, Callaway, did you find a note?"

"A note?"

"Yeah, a suicide note. Did you find one?"

"Not yet. We haven't exactly been looking."

Slopitch sighs. "Well, I guess it's a good thing I decided to drop by."

Sixteen

Slopitch scans the room, nodding to the other cops, until his gaze stops on Pat. "Well, Commander Ryan. You and the legendary Moony together. What is this—a reunion of the Mayor Harold fan club?"

"I see you've finally made detective, Dick. I guess we know whose fan club you've been paying your dues to."

"Nah, I ain't no fan of his. He's got nothing compared to his old man."

Mayor Dickie has not been nearly as effective as his father in courting the police department's support. The thing that pisses the cops off most is that he seems to have given up trying. Which basically means that he doesn't automatically leap to the defense of any cop who's accused of misconduct. He usually waits to see how public opinion is going before taking a stand.

Slopitch motions for the other cops to join him and they move around the corner into the back hallway to confer. I help Jason and Van lift Nelson onto the stretcher. As they start to wheel him out, Slopitch steps back into the room.

"Hey, hold on a second; I want to have a look at him first."

McNulty shakes his head. "Sorry, Detective, we've got to get him to the hospital."

"What's the hurry? The guy's already croaked, right?"

"You know the rules. We've got to take him in. If you want to have a look, you can follow us or visit him at the ME's office."

McNulty shoots me a half-smile and I return it. One of the pleasures of being an EMT is that you have charge of an accident scene over the cops. If a crime is suspected, you do everything you can to preserve the integrity of the crime scene. But saving the victim is your first priority. If Slopitch hadn't come on so strong, I'm sure McNulty would bend the rules for him. But technically, once paramedics are called to a scene and they start life-saving procedures, they're required to transport the victim to a hospital as quickly as possible. They don't have the authority to pronounce someone dead.

Slopitch moves a step toward McNulty and reads his name tag. "Van McNulty. I'll remember you."

McNulty nods. "Actually, we've met before, Detective. I guess you forgot." As he resumes wheeling Nelson out, he looks back over his shoulder. "Call me, Moony, and we'll get a beer."

Slopitch chuckles. "Yeah, or maybe you can smoke some pot together."

Just then, Edith, the clerk from White Hen, returns. "I have the pot right here, officer." Hers contains coffee. "I brought you some doughnuts, too. They're a little old, I'm afraid."

"Thank you," O'Malley says, "don't worry about it."

"Yeah, thanks," Slopitch says. "All cops like doughnuts. Isn't that true, Commander Ryan?"

Pat nods. "It's practically a requirement for the job."

"I'll go and get some more cups." Edith begins counting aloud. She gets to three before she notices that Dr. Nelson is no longer with us. "Where's Edwin—I mean Dr. Nelson?"

"The paramedics took him to the hospital," O'Malley says.

"Hospital?" she looks at me. "You mean he's not dead?"

Slopitch beats me to a response. "Just a formality, Lady. He's not going to be drinking anymore coffee, you can be sure of that." He chuckles and speaks to the group of cops. "Why don't you look around for a note, and one of you call in for a lab tech. And one of you should try and call Dr. Nelson's wife. I assume he's got a wife."

"Oh yes, her name's Abby. She'll be crushed."

"I already called her," Strayhorn says. "She *was* very upset. She's on her way to the hospital."

"You and your partner should go and meet her there. Try and get a statement from her, but go easy." He turns to us. "Are you guys in a hurry to get somewhere, or can you stay and answer a few questions?"

"As long as they're reasonable," Pat says.

"Do I seem unreasonable?" Slopitch grins, and his mouth covers most of his face. "So, the two of you had a meeting with Dr. Nelson."

"That's right, at six-thirty."

"What was the meeting about?"

"Phil had his cat here for the weekend, but when he came to pick him up yesterday, the cat was missing. Nelson told him he had an idea of what'd happened and asked him to come here."

"And why did you come too?"

"I know Nelson a little better. I referred Phil to him."

"I see. And maybe you thought he'd be more willing to answer Moony's questions if you came."

"Yeah, that's the idea, more or less."

"There seems to be some confusion about when you two got here."

"No confusion on our part. We both got here around six-thirty. Phil came in the front, I came in the back."

"You came in the back? Why's that?"

"We already went over this with the uniforms. I've picked

111

up my cats after hours before, and Dr. Nelson leaves the back door open for me."

"And you got here first, is that right, Moony?"

"No," Pat says, "I did."

"Excuse me, Pat, but I think I asked *him* the question, not you."

I know that Pat's intention is to protect me by saying he was there first. But having to remain silent seems to be putting more suspicion on me, not less.

"What is this, Dick? Do you want our cooperation or do you just want to bust our chops?"

Slopitch shrugs. "Okay, so you got here and you saw Nelson on the floor, is that right?"

"Right."

"And then Moony got here like what—a minute later?"

"Yeah—if that." I finally decide to break my silence. But I choose exactly the wrong time to do it.

"Wait, hold on a second, Moony. If you came in after him, then you don't know how long it was after he got here, do you? What's with you guys? You keep answering the other one's questions."

Pat sighs and rolls his eyes, maybe more on my account than because of Slopitch.

I have no trouble working up some exasperation. "Jesus Christ, Slopitch. I come in, I see Pat, I see Nelson on the floor, and we immediately roll him over and start working on him. Okay? That's what happened."

Slopitch raises his hand. "Fine, fine, don't get so upset. So you found him facedown, right?"

"Right," Pat says.

"And you two are the only witnesses?"

"No." Pat points to the cats in the cages. "There were six others."

"Who's busting whose chops now, Commander?" He sighs and stares at me. "I bet you were really pissed off when you came here, Moony."

I shake my head. "I was trying to get my cat back. I didn't see how getting pissed off would help."

"I see. But I'm sure you were feeling pissed. I know I'd be, if the guy lost my cat. Except I don't own a cat, because I hate the damn things. But you didn't threaten him or anything, right? You just came here nice and calm to talk things over, nice and civil, right?"

"Yeah, that's right."

"I see. Hard to believe."

Pat spreads his arms. "What's so hard to believe?"

"Your pal here's known for having a short fuse."

"Who says?" Pat's the one asking.

"I think the fire department's still got the paperwork in his file to show it."

"Let me get this straight. You think Phil got so pissed off about Nelson losing his cat that he killed him? Slopitch, you are really barking up the wrong tree."

"Ha, ha. I get it, Pat. Barking up the wrong tree. Very funny. Actually, I'm thinking about the guy's frame of mind. I'm thinking that if Moony got mad and threatened the guy, maybe he got scared and decided to kill himself."

"I see. The guy's scared Moony's going to come here and kill him, so he does it himself to save him the trouble. Very good theory." Pat looks at me. "Come on, Phil, let's get going. Leave Sherlock to his theorizing."

Slopitch makes a stop sign with his hand. "No, of course I'm not saying that. I'm saying maybe the guy had a whole bunch of personal problems and this thing with Moony was the straw that broke the camel's back." Slopitch waits to get Pat's reaction, but it doesn't come. "You see, Commander, there's something that really puzzles me, something that I think you could help with."

"And just what would that be?"

"The reason I'm asking all these questions is because the coffee lady from White Hen who saw Moony come in here called the cops at six thirty-three. Now you say the two of you got here at the same time—you even a little sooner—but you didn't call nine-one-one until six forty-five. What were you waiting for?"

"We were trying to save the guy's life, for Chrissakes."

"If you were trying to save the guy's life, why didn't you call nine-one-one right away?"

"Because we thought he had a better chance if we tried to revive him."

"Would that be a better chance of living? Or a better chance of dying?"

"Oh, Jesus. Come on, Phil." Pat nods to me, and this time we really do start to leave the room. He waves his hand without looking back. "Nice seeing you again, Dick. Don't forget to send me a Christmas card."

"Detective Slopitch." Callaway appears at the doorway. "We haven't found any suicide note."

"Maybe he forgot to write one. Just like I'm going to do with the commander's Christmas card."

"Huh?" Callaway eyes us quizzically as he steps aside to let us through.

"You know, Patrick, you've got a lot fewer friends downtown than you probably think you've got."

Pat turns to have the last word. "But if I've only got one, that would be one more than you."

"Oh, you're breaking my heart. You guys better hope the ME decides Nelson croaked himself. Because if he doesn't, I'm going to have a lot more questions for you. And you won't be able to just walk away."

As we pass the receptionist desk, Callaway's partner is hanging up the phone.

"Commander Ryan?" She holds out her hand to Pat. As he starts to shake it, she says, "I'm Audrey Carney. Do you remember—Joe Carney's daughter?"

"Oh, Jesus, Mary and Joseph." Pat starts to give her the two-hand treatment. "My, I really am getting old. The last time I saw you, you were . . ."

"Eleven. My confirmation."

"Yes, that's right. With Andy." Pat looks at me. "Audrey was confirmed with my nephew. Her father and I—" He turns back to her. "How is he doing?"

"Well . . . did you hear about the stroke?"

"Yes, I did."

"It was a bad one."

"Yes, that's what I heard."

"He was in rehab but they moved him."

"Where is he?"

"In Niles."

"That's right. The one on Touhy, just east of Milwaukee. I know where it is. The next time you see him, tell him . . . No, don't tell him anything. I'll go see him myself."

"I'd really appreciate that if you would. So would he. I know he would."

"Yes, then I'll do that. I will. It's nice to meet you—I mean see you—again. Good luck."

Pat turns away quickly and moves right for the door. As soon as we step outside, he grips my shoulder. "I want you to make me a promise and I'm going to hold you to it."

"Sure, what's that?"

"If I have a stroke or something and my relatives have gotten together and it looks like I'm on my way to a god-damn nursing home—"

"Shoot you."

"Right. It doesn't have to be with a gun. You can use some of that sodium pento-whatchamacallit."

"Don't worry, Pat. I'll get you something much nicer than that."

Seventeen

We walk right past my car. We both know where we're headed, and it's probably over on Milwaukee Avenue. It's a place called the nearest tavern, and in Chicago you usually don't have to walk more than two blocks to find one.

"Now do you see why I didn't want you to start talking about your suspicions?" Pat says. "I knew you might get someone like Slopitch investigating. You don't want to give a guy like that any ideas. It could hurt his head."

"Sure, I understand that. But if we're the ones who are suggesting that the guy was murdered, isn't that likely to deflect suspicion away from us?"

"To a reasonable person, yes. To a guy like Slopitch, uh-uh."

"You guys really seem to have a hard-on for each other. What's that all about?"

"He used to be on my command. I caught him writing anti-Harold graffiti on the walls in the can. Real vulgar racist stuff."

"Oh, he's the guy. You told me about that."

Pat laughs. "Yeah, he's the guy. I was coming out of the crapper and he's right in the middle of it. I made him scrub every inch of the place and then I sat on a promotion he had coming for almost a year. He hates my guts."

"The feeling seems to be mutual."

"Nah, you don't hate a jerk like that." He begins speaking in a brogue. " 'More to be pitied than scorned,' my mother used to say."

"Aren't you a little concerned that Nelson's death could end up being ruled a suicide when the guy was actually murdered?"

Pat shakes his head. "My concern is finding your cat."

"You mean you don't care about Nelson?"

"No, not particularly. Especially not after what Madge told me about him today. The guy turns out to be a real bastard—he yells at her all the time. Then there's the stuff your sweetie found out about him. He's a scoundrel. So no, I don't care much about him, certainly not as much as I care about your cat. You, on the other hand, seem more concerned about a guy you barely knew."

"It's not that. I just don't want to be responsible for someone getting away with murder."

"Phil, take my word for it. The moment the medical examiner sees the marks on Nelson's arms, he's going to know it wasn't a suicide. Which means that Slopitch will be back at us with a vengeance."

"Oh, you noticed those too?"

"Please, give me a break. I was born at night, but it wasn't last night."

"Well, then why didn't you notice *these?*" I stop and hold my hands out in front of me.

"Why didn't I notice what?"

"I'm still wearing Nelson's gloves."

"Oh, Jesus."

I'm about to start laughing, but I'm not sure Pat will see any humor in it.

"Why the hell didn't *you* notice?"

"I don't know. I forgot I had them on."

"You are one goddamn menace to the integrity of a crime scene. Do you realize that?"

I shrug. "I'm just having a bad night."

"I'll say. You're giving me one hell of a bad night too."

"Sorry. What do we do?"

He looks over his shoulder at the Purr & Bark office. "One thing we don't do: We don't go back inside and give them to Slopitch. Although it would almost be worth it, just to see the look on his face."

"Could we give them to Audrey?"

"That's not a bad idea." He shakes his head. "No. Send her in to face Slopitch? I can't do that to the daughter of a friend of mine. I wouldn't do that to the daughter of an enemy of mine."

He rubs his hand through the few silver strands of hair that he has left and yawns. "Let me think about this for a minute." He does his thinking aloud, but it's a mumble, not intended for me to respond to. "If the ME thinks Nelson was not wearing gloves, then he'll wonder why his prints aren't on the syringe. He might think that someone wiped them off, which will make him suspect homicide. But if he thinks Nelson wasn't wearing gloves, he may wonder why there isn't any DNA stuff under his fingernails from clawing at his attacker, which might make him lean toward suicide. But of course there just might be some DNA if the killer is the one who put the gloves on Nelson, thinking that would be a way to not leave any prints on the syringe and not arouse suspicion. *If* the killer thought about it that much—which he probably didn't, otherwise he wouldn't have been dumb enough to leave the syringe in Nelson's hand in the first place."

He throws up his arms. "Oh, Lord, get me to a tavern fast. I'd say it's a wash. Throw them in the next goddamn dumpster we come to, and don't look back. And don't ever get me into another mess like this again. And . . ."

"Yes?"

"You're buying."

"Naturally."

I buy several of them for each of us. Beers to start with, but we work our way into shots of Jägermeister, which is a drink that Pat's nephew has recently introduced him to. It was part of his first-semester curriculum at Notre Dame, and Pat is a sucker for anything having to do with Notre Dame. He says it's strong evidence that "you can teach an old dog new tricks."

That may be the case for him, but when morning rolls around, I can't even get my wife to roll over. Playing dead is the only trick she seems to know after a night out with Charlotte Penske, and there's nothing new about that.

I'm up at the crack of dawn, at least by my standards. I do my morning waltz—shower, coffee, newspaper—on tiptoe, and manage to get a cup poured and deposited on her night table without spilling it.

The aroma of the coffee does it. Frankie wakes by sense of smell, not hearing.

"How did it go with Nelson last night?" She speaks with her eyes closed and her mouth against her pillow.

"It didn't go at all."

"What's that supposed to mean?"

"Someone killed him."

"What?" She sits upright in an instant, but a sickly look spreads over her face. In another, her head's back on the pillow.

"I guess you had a rough night with Charlotte, huh?"

"We had a lot of laughs. I'm still willing to pay the price for them." Her voice is husky, even by her usual morning standards. "But the price keeps getting steeper as I get older.

"I guess you had a lot of smokes last night too."

"Yeah, yeah. Don't nag."

"I'm not nagging, I'm just observing."

"Then try to be a little less observant. And no more jokes

the morning after to get my attention. You know how gullible I can be."

"I'm not joking. Nelson's really dead."

"What do you mean? What happened?" This time she remains prone.

"Someone killed him and tried to make it look like suicide."

"How'd they do that?"

"Remember what we were going to do to Phull last Friday afternoon? Someone did that to Dr. Nelson."

"Our vet was euthanized?"

"Yup. By either two people or one very strong son of a bitch."

"Muscle Boy Rod and Dear Abby."

"Motive?"

"She wants longer workouts, he wants more money."

"Now, now, don't jump to conclusions, sweetheart. I've got to go, but you can read all about it in here." I toss the *Sun-Times* onto the bed.

"Nelson's dead, and you were there, and you're not going to stay and tell me about it?"

"I can probably get home by lunchtime." I lean down and give her a kiss. "Maybe we can have lunch together."

"Sure, I'll make some Spaghetti-O's for you."

I start toward the doorway and point to the paper, "It's on page *cinquantanove*."

"*Lo apri tu. Sono stanca.*"

"Beg your pardon? Excuse me, I mean, '*Scusa*.'"

"I said, 'You open it. I'm too tired.'"

She gets into a half-sitting position—at least her head is propped against the wall, and her knees are up—to receive the paper, which I drop gently on her midsection.

"NORTHWEST SIDE VET FOUND DEAD." She clears her throat, and her voice rises a few notes. "A Northwest Side veterinarian was found dead in his Jefferson Park office Tuesday evening."

"You don't have to read it out loud. I read it already."

"Oh, but I like to. It's more dramatic that way." She takes a mouthful of coffee. "Eighteenth District police said Edwin Nelson, owner of the Purr & Bark veterinary clinic in the fifty-one hundred block of West Lawrence Avenue, was found on the floor of his office around seven o'clock by two customers." She looks at me over the edge of the paper. "Anyone I know?"

I answer with a smile.

"They attempted CPR but were unsuccessful. Paramedics took him to Our Lady of the Resurrection Hospital, where he was pronounced dead. Police said the cause of death was unknown but foul play is not suspected at this time."

She closes the paper. "Well, it sounds like the police and you don't agree on the cause of death."

"I think the key words there are 'at this time.' They will, once the medical report comes in. There was a detective from Violent Crimes there, and he was trying to put us through the ringer."

"Pat too?"

"Yeah. Him especially. They know each other. And they don't like each other." I look at the clock. "Honey, I've really got to go."

"Where are you going?"

"To meet Pat. We're going to talk to some of the customers who were at the vet's office Monday morning, when Phull got snatched. I don't want to keep him waiting."

"It's not like he expects you to be on time. He knows you better than that."

"Hey, guess what. I was on time last night. He was late. Of all the nights to get someplace ahead of him."

"You were there first?" She sits up, for real. "You were alone when you found Nelson?"

"Yeah. But unfortunately, Pat told the cops he got there first—as a way of protecting me."

"Why is that a problem? He's just being paternalistic."

"Because I started in doing CPR on the guy right away. Dad didn't call nine-one-one until about ten minutes later. So this cop is wondering why he took so long."

"I don't understand. How did he know when you got there?"

"I told him."

"Such an honest man I married."

"Yeah, and it's a good thing. Because a woman saw me going in and called the cops to report a prowler."

"You're kidding. Who was it?"

"A clerk at the White Hen."

"A clerk at a White Hen noticed something and called the cops? They're asleep half the time I'm in there."

"I think she was probably on her cigarette break." I look at the clock once more. I'm definitely not going to break my consecutive number of times on time record. "I'm telling you so much, there's going to be nothing to tell you at lunchtime."

She shrugs. "Then don't come home then."

"But I was so looking forward to the Spaghetti-O's."

"How about if I make you a frozen pizza for dinner?"

Eighteen

Pat is standing outside the Dunkin' Donuts on Addison Street, holding two coffees.

"I didn't think you could be on time twice in a row."

"I've got a wife I have to talk to in the morning."

"Don't make it sound like it's a chore. You're lucky to have her."

"I know that. That's why I make a point of talking to her."

"If I were married to a woman as beautiful as your wife, I'd be doing a lot more than talking, let me tell you."

"Guys like you—that's why they have mutual-consent laws."

"Well, I've got five cats to feed before I get out the door, so there's still no excuse."

"Five? I thought you had four."

"Yeah, I do. I'm watching one for somebody."

"Who's that?"

"A neighbor. We'll take my car. Park yours around the corner on Kimball and I'll pick you up."

When I get in, Pat hands me a sheet of paper with six names and addresses on it. One of the addresses is a firehouse, Engine Company 106, at 3401 North Elston. That goes with the name at the top of the list.

"First stop, Mr. David Zezel, one of your former EMT brethren. Do you know the guy?"

"Yeah, but not very well. I can't imagine the guy would be holding a grudge against me. Although . . ."

"Although what?"

"Someone once told me he made a crack about me and Frankie. It was during the Mayor Harold campaign. And I think he might be a friend of Ron Ostrow's."

"Well, any guy who makes a crack about your wife deserves to be regarded with plenty of suspicion. A crack about you, I can understand. So, what did Frankie say when you told her about Nelson?"

"She thinks the doctor was done in by his wife and her personal trainer."

"And she's probably right."

"You haven't even met them."

"No, but I heard your story about them, and Madge tells me the wife is a monster."

"She told you Dr. Nelson was something of a monster too."

"That's right. They were probably monsters to each other."

"But do you think she killed him because of my cat?"

"If she's the one who snatched Phull and he was threatening to do something to her about it, yeah, that's possible. If she isn't, you mentioned he was planning on shutting down her breeding operation. The husband or wife is always a suspect. People kill the ones they love because they hate them so damn much."

We park at the corner of Roscoe. As we begin our approach to the big, wide-open garage doors, I start to get the shivers. I used to feel so comfortable walking into any firehouse, but now I'm an outsider. It's not just that I no longer have an official reason for being there that bothers me. At some of them, I'm downright unwelcome. As far as I know, this isn't one of them. But I could be wrong.

As we step inside, we see a guy who's too fat to slide down a fire pole hanging on the side of a truck, polishing the mirror. Pat tells him we're looking for Dave Zezel, and he shouts to someone who's out of our sight.

"Hey, Larry, where's Z-Man?"

I now remember that Zezel, like practically every other guy whose name begins with Z, goes by the moniker Z-Man. And as Larry steps out from behind the truck to answer, I remember him as someone I don't particularly like. I can't remember why and I can't remember his last name, but as he looks at me, I'm pretty sure the feeling's mutual.

"He went out to his car to get his smokes," Larry says, pointing past us to the street. "Why—is there a problem?"

"Nope, no problem," Pat says. "We just wanted to talk to him for a minute."

We turn and start down Elston, and I can feel Larry's eyes boring a hole in my back. It occurs to me that I'm being paranoid, but when I glance over my shoulder to check, I can see Larry glowering at us with hands on hips.

Zezel is standing on the sidewalk next to a white Pontiac Firebird about half a block down the street, lighting a cigarette. I can tell it's his car because of the license plate: ZMAN.

"Phil Moony, what are you doing here?"

"Hey, Z, I came by to talk to you."

"Is it about your cat?"

I nod. "Yeah, how did you know?"

"Somebody tipped me off." He exhales a cloud of smoke and watches it disappear. "Ron Ostrow. I saw him on a run yesterday. He says you went off on him, says you accused him of stealing your cat, says you threatened to kill him."

"Uh, that's not exactly what happened. In fact, it's not even close."

"Yeah, well, Ronnie tends to exaggerate a lot. He's kind

of an excitable boy. Especially lately. I hear he's got a little mid-life crisis going on the side. A nurse. I don't know if you noticed, but he's really bulked up. But I think that's got more to do with you than her."

"Me?"

"Sure, you know. He's scared shit of you, ever since . . ."

"Oh, I see. That wasn't my finest hour."

Zezel shrugs. "Well, he had it coming to him."

"Why do you say that?"

"He set you up, didn't he?"

"Did he tell you that?"

"Whoa." Zezel raises his hands in defense. "I'm not touching that one. That was just the word going around. And anybody with five brain cells could figure out it wasn't a coincidence. You had enemies in high places, Moony."

I nod but don't break the uncomfortable silence. It's nice to learn you have an unexpected ally after the fact, but there's nothing to be gained by going over it all again.

"So, we all have the same vet," Zezel says. "Is that a coincidence, or what?"

"*Had* the same vet." Pat extends his hand. "Pat Ryan. I used to be on the police department."

"Yeah, I think I remember," Zezel says, shaking it. "You got pretty close to the top of the heap, didn't you?"

"Area commander."

"Well, that's something to write home about. And now you're retired and helping guys find their lost pets. I can't wait until my twenty years are up."

"Dr. Nelson's dead," Pat says.

"Really? Are you shitting me?" Zezel takes a last drag, then flicks his cigarette into the street. "Damn, there goes my free vet services."

"Yeah, a lot of us have that problem now," Pat says.

"Oh, you too? I guess we'll have to put out an all-points bulletin. 'Cops and firemen looking for a vet who won't charge.' " Zezel laughs and begins walking back to the firehouse. "What did you do, Moony? Croak the guy for losing your cat?"

"No, it was a do-it-yourselfer. I found the guy, and Van McNulty took him in."

"Well, with you and McNulty on the case, it's no wonder he didn't make it."

"We talked to the receptionist at Nelson's office," Pat said. "She thought you were there the morning someone picked up Phil's cat. The guy—"

Zezel stops in his tracks. "What? When?"

"Monday morning."

"This past Monday? She's full of shit."

"Hey, take it easy. We're not accusing you of stealing Phil's cat," Pat says. "The guy who picked him up had a badge. We thought you might remember seeing him."

Zezel starts walking again. "I haven't been there for a couple of months at least. Sorry I can't help you."

"I guess she must have been mistaken," Pat says.

"Yeah, very mistaken. Which one was it—the old bag or the wife?"

"Nelson's wife," Pat says.

"Well, her I can forgive. Her, I wouldn't throw out of bed for eating crackers. She said the guy who took your cat was on the fire department?"

"It could be the cops," I say. "She just knew he had a badge."

"Star or shield?"

"She didn't notice."

"I guess she's a real brain trust, huh. Well, I still wouldn't throw her out of bed for eating crackers. It sounds like you've still got your enemies, Moony." We're back at the doors to the firehouse, and he holds out his hand to shake. "I'll keep my ears open and let you know if I hear anything."

"Thanks a lot, Z. I'd appreciate that."

"Commander." Zezel holds out his hand to Pat, who's

about to turn away. "If you get a line on a vet who doesn't charge, be sure and let me know."

"Yeah, you'll be the second guy I call."

"Who'll be the first?"

"Moony's other Pal—Ostrow."

Pat turns abruptly away, and Zezel shoots me a puzzled look. All I can do is shrug and try to keep up with him.

Nineteen

I take it you didn't like that guy very much."

"You're wrong, I didn't like him at all," Pat says. "I thought you said you didn't know him very well."

"I don't."

"Seems like he was being awful buddy-buddy with you."

"Yeah, I kind of thought that too. Did Madge tell you that Zezel was in the office the morning Phull was snatched?"

"No. I just said that to get a reaction from him. And it worked, did you notice? He stopped the wise-guy crap right away."

"So, do you think he's our catnapper?"

"Too early to tell. Let's see what these other folks have to say."

They're all within a couple of miles of Nelson's office, so it's not hard to cover them in the space of the morning. We don't learn anything about Phull's whereabouts from the next four on the list, but I do discover that my cat is the epitome of neatness compared with the ravages that some pets have visited upon their owner's homes. By the time we get through, I've seen enough cat hair and dog hair and soiled carpets and stinky litter boxes and spilled water bowls and moldy dishes of pet food to last nine lifetimes. And I'm ready to pass on the last name on Pat's list, Millicent Melrose.

"Nope," Pat says, "we've got to check them all. Besides, how can you pass on a name like that? My guess is Millicent's a cat person. What do you think?"

I nod in agreement. I'm thinking the name fits the multiple-cat profile, but I don't mention this to Pat. After all, he's got four of the little buggers himself.

It turns out Millicent has quintuplets, though only four are presently home. It's a wonder she can fit them all in her house. It's the smallest model of Chicago bungalow, the kind that's designed for childless couples under five feet tall. When it comes to living space, the lady who lived in a shoe had a leg up on Millicent.

She's a feisty little number, a widow going on ten years, she tells us early on. She meets the residency requirements with half a foot to spare. She's wearing a pink bathrobe, pink slippers, eyeglasses with pink frames and a pink bow in her hair, which is silver with blue highlights or maybe vice versa. The walls of her little abode are painted pink, and the carpet would still be pink if it weren't for the five cats, who apparently have an aversion to litter boxes.

She's feeding them lunch when we arrive, and she offers to feed us too. We tell her not to go to any trouble, but she points out how little trouble it would be to make tuna fish for two more. She seems disappointed, so we let her serve us tea.

"Oh, yes, Dr. Nelson," she says, as she puts the tray on the coffee table in front of the pink couch. She picks up a romance novel and stashes it in the pocket of her robe. "I'm very mad at Dr. Nelson, you know."

"Why's that?" Pat asks.

"I have to make two trips to pick up my Lola. I had her in getting fixed. When it comes to neutering, I'm kind of old-fashioned. I had it done with Lena, Lana and Lulu— they're my females. But I don't neuter my tom. They're all my girlfriends, but Ralph is my main squeeze, I suppose you could say." She holds her hand down near the floor, and an orange tabby saunters over. He's a fat cat, but not in Bobo's weight division. "It's so nice to have a man around the house."

We smile and nod and Pat asks again why she's annoyed at Edwin Nelson.

"As I told you, because I have to make two trips. I have to go back there and pick her up today. I was supposed to get her yesterday afternoon. But when I got there, the door was locked. And it was only ten minutes before six."

"Are you sure?"

"I'm positive. I know because my watch said six o'clock and I always set it ten minutes fast so that I won't be late."

"Did you ring the bell? They have a bell there."

"Yes, I rang the bell. But no one answered."

"Hmm, that's strange."

"That's what I thought. And when I go back there today, I'm going to give Dr. Nelson a piece of my mind. With my arthritis, it's not easy to go to the vet."

"I'm sure it's not. I know when mine starts acting up, I have trouble just feeding the cats, no less taking them to the vet."

"Exactly. So you have cats too?"

"Yup, four of them. But I have some bad news for you. Dr. Nelson died yesterday."

"Noooo!"

"I'm afraid so."

"What happened?"

"It looks like he killed himself."

Millicent nods. "I knew it."

"You knew what?"

"I knew he wasn't a happy man. It's that wife of his. She's such a tart. A wife like that can cause a man a lot of heartache."

Pat nods knowingly, as if he once had a wife like that.

134

Just then one of the cats comes over and hops up onto his lap.

"Oh, Lana, you're such a flirt. If she's bothering you, you can put her down."

"Not at all. But it's not Dr. Nelson or my cats that we're here for, Mrs. Melrose."

"Please, call me Millicent."

"Millicent. We're here because someone stole Mr. Moony's cat from Nelson's office on Monday morning, around the time you were there."

"That's terrible. What kind was it?"

"A Maine coon," I say.

"Oh, I love them. They're so adorable. And I remember. But I just can't believe it."

"You can't believe what, Mrs. Melrose?"

"Millicent, please."

Pat smiles. "Millicent. What is it that you can't believe?"

"The man who took Mr. Moony's cat. He seemed like such a nice young man."

"You saw him?"

"Oh yes. He was very handsome. And muscular. He must be a weight lifter. And he was very nice. He held the door for me when I was leaving and he told me to have a nice day. Young men don't do that anymore, you know. They don't hold doors and they don't wish you a nice day."

"Yes, I know, it's a shame. How young a man was he?"

"About Mr. Moony's age, I'd say. Twenty-five."

"You're very kind," I say. It so happens I'm staring down the barrel at forty, coming at me next April first. My father, according to my mother, wondered if they should call me Phool Moony. "And you know what?" she told me one of the last times I saw her. "I think he might have been right." Mom was my biggest booster, but she was also my hardest critic.

Pat shoots me a grin. "Can you tell us what this young man about Mr. Moony's age looked like?"

"I already told you, he was handsome and muscular and tall."

"Like Mr. Moony."

"Yes."

"Do you remember what color hair he had?"

"I really couldn't tell. It was short. He was wearing a baseball cap. He had it on backwards. Why do they wear it like that, do you know?" She's asking me, being the young one.

I shake my head. "Beats me."

"We didn't talk long. He wished me a nice day and then he drove away in a white sports car. Do you want to know the license plate?"

"Do you know it?" Pat asks, shooting me another look.

"The letters, not the numbers. It was ZA. That's library science and information."

"I beg your pardon?"

"Library science and information. It's the Library of Congress classification. I always remember license plate letters because I think of their library classification. I was the librarian at Wildwood School until three years ago. Thirty-five years. I'm better with the Dewey decimal system. I use that for remembering phone numbers."

"Wonderful." Pat begins to rise from the couch, with Lana clinging to him. "Millicent, you've been a tremendous amount of help."

"You're going already? You don't have any more questions?"

"I have one," I say. "Are you sure the license plate wasn't ZMAN?" I'm thinking I'd like to head right back to the firehouse and take a baseball bat to Dave Zezel's pride and joy, and maybe to Zezel himself.

She shakes her head. "No, that wouldn't be library science and information."

"I see." I pick up the tray off the table and start for the kitchen.

"Don't bother, I can do that," she says, reaching out for the tray. "But it's so nice of you to help."

"I hold doors for ladies and wish them a nice day, too."

"I'll bet you do. Your wife is a lucky woman." She looks at Pat. "And yours too, Patrick."

"I'm not married."

She nods solemnly. "Widowed?"

"Nope, never been there or done that."

"Now how could that be?" The tray wobbles as she shakes her head, and Pat reaches out to steady it. "Thank you. I'm sorry you couldn't stay longer. If you have any more questions . . ."

"Oh, yes, we may."

Millicent's face brightens at the prospect of another visit.

"And since you've been so helpful," Pat says, "and considering your arthritis and all, how about it if I pick up Lola for you?"

"Oh, no, please don't trouble yourself."

"It's no trouble. I've got to go by Nelson's office anyway."

"Would you really do that for me?"

"I'd be happy to."

She's beaming as she and Ralph watch us all the way to our car from the steps. As we pull away, I see her pull the book she was reading from her pocket.

"You made an old lady very happy, Commander Ryan," I say.

"She's not that old. And she made me very happy. I think we may have your cat back by tonight."

"Well, what now? Are we going over to see Dave Zezel and give him a going-over?"

Pat shakes his head. "We better make sure we have the right guy first."

"I wouldn't call Zezel handsome, but he's solidly built. And he's got a white sports car with Z and A on the license plates. That's not enough?"

"You said Abby Nelson's personal trainer was a Mr. Universe type. She could have handed Phull over to him and told you it was a cop just to make you nervous. As far as the license plate goes, Millicent seemed pretty certain it was ZA, not ZMAN. There are still a few unmarked squads left with ZA plates."

"Really? I haven't seen any." ZA used to be the designation on all unmarked Chicago police cars. Which basically meant that there was no such thing as an unmarked car. Not that it's gotten much harder to spot them nowadays. They're all white Chevy Caprices, and they usually have a pair of clean-cut beefy guys doing their awkward best to look scraggly. The FBI had the same problem infiltrating the anti-war movement on college campuses in the late sixties. Not many kids in Madison wore suits to classes.

"You still see them around once in a while."

"I'm sure she's no car expert, but I doubt even Millicent would mistake a squad car for a sports car."

Pat shrugs. "You never know. She mistook you for a young man."

"And you for a polite one."

"That's right. We may be seeing Zezel pretty soon, but let's get some more to go on first."

Twenty

We part company back at my car. Pat's heading for the vet's office. I'm heading for home. He's eager to see what's cooking in Dr. Nelson's absence. I'm eager to find out what Frankie's cooked up for lunch.

Pat expects to find Madge in charge, and he intends to ask her about the office being locked when Millicent Melrose was there yesterday. He also wants to find out if Slopitch has been sniffing around asking questions yet. And, of course, there's the matter of picking up Millicent's cat.

"Good luck," I say. "I hope nobody snatched it."

"Hey, don't even joke about that. I'll talk to you tonight."

"Do you have plans for this afternoon?"

"Don't bother asking." When Pat says that, it often means he's about to save you the bother by answering before you can ask. "I'll be spending the whole damn afternoon visiting a guy in a nursing home. That's if I'm lucky. If I'm not lucky, I'll only stay a few minutes and I'll spend the rest of the afternoon feeling guilty for not going to see the guy sooner."

I think of Albie, and the long afternoons he and I spent

together in his final days. I advise Pat to take a deck of cards along.

"Cards? Phil, I really doubt this guy's got anything close to a full deck left."

"The cards aren't for him, they're for you."

"Oh, I get it. Solitaire confinement. Maybe I'll just bring a string of rosary beads and see if I can remember the words to the Hail Mary."

"Patrick, there's a special place in heaven for you."

"Yeah, sure. Last row, second balcony." He puts out his hand. "Maybe your wife has a special place set for you at the lunch table."

Hardly. It turns out I have the same menu option that I turned down at the Melrose place. I only eat tuna fish maybe once a year, but Frankie and Phull, they love the stuff. She's hungry for information about Dr. Nelson, and she has a few morsels of her own to feed to me.

"This came twenty minutes ago," she says, holding an envelope from Federal Express. "Someone went to a big expense to send you this little note."

The message is hand printed and fits on a three-by-five index card with plenty to room to spare:

SAY GOOD-BYE TO YOUR CAT JAGOFF.
HOW DOES IT FEEL?

I check the envelope. "Hey, it's addressed to me. Don't I get to open my own mail?" I feign indignation, but she knows I'm kidding.

"When I saw the return address, I decided not to wait."

In the sender's box is the name Dolly Katz. The street line says 9 Litterbox Lane. The rest of it is straight Chicago, with a Northwest Side zip code.

"Do you think there's a way to trace it?" I ask.

"I already did. It got sent from one of those 'We pack it, ship it, and charge you a dollar an inch for the Scotch tape' stores. This one's called 'We-Mail.' It's on Lawrence, a couple of blocks west of Milwaukee." She hands me the address, which she has written on a WYWFO note, which is our acronym for the WHILE YOU WERE FUCKING OFF memo pads that some of my fire-department pals gave me as a going-away present.

"Which puts it a couple of doors east of Scratch & Sniff," I say.

"Gosh, you're right. That means the guy who snatched Phull had the gall to return to the scene of the crime. He probably lives near there."

"Or works near there."

"Do you mean Madge, the receptionist?"

"Madge isn't a guy. I was thinking of the cop shop right there on Milwaukee. And there's a firehouse two blocks down Milwaukee at Wilson." I study the message before putting it in my pocket. "What do you make of the greeting: 'How does it feel?'"

"I'd say it was written by someone who doesn't like you very much and hasn't liked you for a very long time."

"That would eliminate Abby Nelson from consideration."

She nods. "I hate to admit it, but I think you're right. Only a native Chicagoan uses the word 'jagoff,' and Abby, we've learned, is from another planet."

"Which part do you hate—that I'm right about something, or that Abby isn't the perp?"

"About Abby, of course. I love it when you're right, darling. I also love it when you use cop lingo. It's so . . . manly." She feigns a swoon and falls into my arms. "It's so nice being married to a man who watches all the cop shows on TV."

"That experience should benefit me when I try to get a line on the suspect from the We-Mail people."

"Are you going there right away?"

"No, first I thought I'd fill you in on what Pat and I found out. And I think I should make a phone call."

"Convey your condolences to the merry widow?"

"Come on now. The lady's in mourning."

"That probably means she's having Mr. Universe put her through a double workout."

"You know, sweetheart, sometimes you can be very . . ."

"Catty, perhaps?"

"Perhaps."

"Meow."

After remarking on the restorative benefits of a little hair of the dog, Frankie curls up on the sofa with a glass of wine. I start in briefing her on the morning's doings. By the time I'm done, she says through a yawn that she's about ready for a catnap. This has less to do with the quality of my narrative than with the quantity of her high jinks with Charlotte last night.

As soon as Frankie dozes off, I seize the opportunity to call Abby Nelson. If she were awake, she'd hover by the phone and make editorial commentary.

"Phil, it's so nice of you to call. I really appreciate it." Abby's voice is not lacking any of its usual sleepiness, but I don't hear anything in her tone to suggest that she's depressed about her husband's demise. "Did you find Edwin yet?"

"I beg your pardon?"

"Your cat. Edwin."

"No, I didn't. But I think we're making some progress."

"That's good. Well, the police told me that you found Edwin."

"My cat?"

"No. My husband. The big-game eater."

"Uh, yes, that's right, I did."

"I'm sorry to sound so sarcastic, but things were not going very well between my husband and myself. He was very moody and unhappy. I can't say I'm really shocked that he did it. He threatened to on more than one occasion. The thing that surprises me most is that he actually went through with it. I didn't think he had the . . ."

Balls is the word that comes immediately to my mind, but I'm not about to fill in any blanks for the woman. I also have no interest in dissuading her from the belief that her husband killed himself. That may be what she wants to believe, or it may be what she wants me to believe.

". . . the nerve," she says, completing the thought. "Phil, do I sound cold and indifferent to you? I hope not. Because I'm really a nice person. I really am. I hope you can believe that."

"Yes, I'm sure you are, Abby. And no, you don't sound cold to me. You sound angry."

"Angry. That's it exactly, Phil. Edwin has left me with a terrible mess to straighten out and I . . . well, I guess I'm very lonely too. I mean I have Bobo, but . . . well, I have Bobo, and we're going to be fine. Ishn't that right, Shweetie? Yesh, it is."

"Well, Abby, I just wanted to call and offer my condolences. I don't know if there's anything I can do, but—"

"Yes, Phil, there is something."

I was afraid she might say that. I brace myself for what's coming, hoping it's not a dinner invitation. "Yes, what is it?"

"Could you tell me, did Edwin speak to you before he died? Did he have anything to say?"

In other circumstances, it would be a very reasonable question. Almost everyone I've spoken to after being unable to resuscitate a loved one has asked me the same thing. Not that it's happened that many times. Maybe a dozen in my twelve years on the fire department. But coming from Abby Nelson, I have some suspicions about why she's asking. It's possible she wants to know if her husband had any last message that he wanted to leave for her. More likely, she's worried that he might have pointed to her as the person who jabbed a lethal needle into his arm.

"No, Abby, I'm sorry, he didn't. I did everything I could to save him, but I'm afraid I got there too late."

"Yes, I'm sure you did. You're a good person, Phil, I can tell that. Which is why I think I should warn you."

"Warn me about what?"

"The police were here this morning asking questions. Two detectives—a man with a lady partner. I wrote their names down, but I don't—"

"Slopitch," I said.

"Yes, that's it. That's the man's name. He said they're looking into the possibility that Edwin was murdered. I told him I thought that was crazy, that Edwin was very depressed, just like I told you. He was asking all sorts of questions about who might have wanted him dead, and he kept asking about you and Mr. Ryan. But mostly he was asking about you. It seemed very clear to me that he doesn't like you, Phil."

She pauses, waiting for my reaction. I don't give her one.

"I told him I was sure you were upset about missing your little Edwin, but not enough to kill my Edwin. He asked if you had threatened Edwin, and I told him I was sure you hadn't, that in fact you seemed very calm and reasonable for a person in your position. And I didn't say anything about your wife. I decided to keep her out of it."

"Thank you, I appreciate that."

"Of course. I also told him about some people back in Ohio who lost their cats that Edwin was having trouble with. Those are the lawsuits still pending against us. And there was a man in Chicago whose cat died with us last year. He was very angry and he did threaten to kill Edwin. I told them I might be able to find the name in the files, but Madge does such a terrible job keeping the records, who knows? But he didn't seem interested in that. He only seemed interested in you. I almost got the feeling he was out to get you, Phil."

"I don't know about that. But I'm not the most popular guy with the Chicago police, that's for sure."

"Why is that?"

"It's a very long story, Abby."

There's a long pause, and I think she may be waiting for

me to begin. Then she sighs. "Well, maybe sometime, when all this is over, you can tell me about it. I'm a good listener, Phil."

"I'm sure you are."

"It's just not fair. You try to save Edwin's life, and then they go and accuse you of killing him. Would you like me to call someone for you and complain?"

"No, it's all right; please don't do that. You're very busy and going through a very hard time." I don't see any point in telling her that it wouldn't do any good, and that it might make the cops think we were in on it together. The newspaper headline writers could have a lot of fun with that one. I repeat myself, with some urgency this time. "Please don't."

"Well, okay, if you say so."

"Oh, there goes the doorbell. I'm sorry. I've got to go." That's a lie. I really don't. Our doorbell has never worked. I don't think I've had a working doorbell anywhere I've lived. But I want out of this conversation, now. "We'll talk again. And I'm sorry for your loss."

"Soon, I hope."

"Yes, soon." I hope not.

Twenty-one

If my mother were still alive, she'd say God punished me. God punished me for telling a lie, even if it was just a little white one, even to someone as strange as Abby Nelson.

But damn if I don't see someone coming up the walk, about ten seconds away from ringing our bum doorbell, when I go back to the living room to check on Frankie. She's moved from catlike dozing into full-bore bear slumber, which means she growls and kicks and glowers when I wake her to give her the news.

"Rise up angry, honey. We've got company."

"What?"

"There's someone at the door."

"I hate it when people just drop by without calling. Don't answer it. Tell them to go away."

"These folks never call in advance."

"Who is it?"

Detective Dick Slopitch answers her question before I can. In the process he proves he can shout and knock at the same time. "Chicago police!"

"Oh, no." Frankie shakes her head.

"Oh, yes."

"Do you want me to call Burt?" Burt Levison is our lawyer.

"Uh yes, uh no. I don't know. You decide. But call Pat, okay? No, Pat's out all afternoon."

Slopitch knocks again. "Phil Moony, we'd like to ask you a few questions."

"No, don't call anyone. Just stay here with me, okay?" I reach out and touch her hand before I start toward the door.

"Of course."

"Will you take notes?"

"Of course."

Slopitch is wearing a smirk that takes up most of the doorway. His partner fills the rest. She's plump, in her forties and as plain as a vanilla wafer. Her name is Candy Clay. Slopitch makes the introduction after I agree to let them in. I don't bother introducing Frankie and she doesn't introduce herself. She just sits on the couch, pen poised over a steno pad, still glowering.

"Mr. Moony, we just have a few questions, won't take up much of your time." Slopitch waits for an acknowledgment from me, continues when he doesn't get one. "Last night, you said you weren't mad at Dr. Nelson, you said you were just going to sit down and have a meeting with him. But that's not what his receptionist said. She said you were furious."

I'm a bit startled by the charge, but I try not to let on. I thought I was rather patient when Madge was there, but I did lose my temper a little.

"We also spoke to Edwin Nelson's wife this morning. She had quite a little story to tell about you. She says you threatened to kill her husband over losing your cat. She says he was terrified of you. She says you came out to her house looking for your cat and threatened her too."

I stare straight at Slopitch but don't say a word.

"Well, what do you have to say?"

"Is that your question?"

117

Slopitch throws back his head. "Oh, we're going to play it this way. Moony, did you threaten Edwin Nelson?"

"No."

"Did you threaten his wife?"

"No."

"So you're saying she's lying."

I shrug. "One of you is."

"What's that supposed to mean?"

"I think you can figure it out." I look at his partner. "Ms. Clay, did Abby Nelson really say those things about me?"

Clay ignores me and steps toward Frankie. "Excuse me. Are you taking notes?"

"Yes, I am." Frankie doesn't look up.

"I really don't think that's necessary."

Frankie nods but keeps writing. "Thanks for the advice."

Clay looks at Slopitch.

He shrugs. "See, what did I tell you?"

He's baiting us, but I can't ignore it. "What did you tell her?"

"About what a nice couple you are."

"How would you know?"

"Oh, you know, you hear things."

"Yeah, I know. I've heard some dandy stuff about you."

"Is that so?"

"So, are you done with your questions?"

"Just about. So you're saying the receptionist is lying too? You weren't angry?"

"I wasn't pleased but I wasn't angry. And I didn't threaten him."

"Okay, if that's what you say. But I can tell you, if the guy lost my cat, I sure would've been pissed off at him. I might've even threatened him. But not you, Moony. You're just a polite, easygoing guy, right?"

Frankie finally speaks up. I know it's been killing her to have to bite her tongue. "Detective Clay, how carefully did you talk to Dr. Nelson's new widow? She's got a young stud boyfriend. And her husband was about to make her get rid of all her cats. It wouldn't take a genius to figure out that she's the one who did it."

Slopitch grins. "You know, Mrs. Moony, believe it or not, that did cross my mind as a possibility. But you know what? It didn't happen. One of the officers at the scene last night phoned Mrs. Nelson to let her know about her husband. And she was home, in Winnetka. She answered the phone. That was shortly before seven o'clock. Now the receptionist didn't leave the office until six-fifteen. If Mrs. Nelson killed her husband, there's no way she could've gotten home to answer the call."

Frankie waves the air with her hand. "Winnetka's not that far. She could have made it."

"During rush hour?"

"Rush hour's over by then."

"Have you been on the Edens Expressway lately? It's under construction. And another thing: Tuesday night, a truck overturned. All lanes were closed. The highway was a parking lot. The picture was on the front page of both the papers. I guess maybe you don't read the papers."

Anyone else would be deflated by that revelation. I know I am. But Frankie, she's tenacious.

"She didn't have to do it herself. She could have hired someone. And there also are people in Ohio who lost their cats when Nelson worked out there. I suggest you look at them."

"Yes, we know all about them. And there's one other in Chicago too. Mrs. Nelson told us, so did the receptionist. Unless, of course"—he looks at me—"they were lying." He turns back to Frankie and smiles. "So, don't worry, Mrs. Moony, we're checking out everything thoroughly."

Frankie's getting flustered but she's keeping her composure. "Well, maybe you'll think about checking into this." She turns and heads into the dining room. A moment later she returns with the anonymous note we received. She hands it to Slopitch, who looks it over and passes it to his partner.

"We're Violent Crimes, not Missing Pets, Mrs. Moony. Maybe your friend Pat Ryan could help you crack the case. He's supposed to be a good detective."

Frankie glares. "Better than you'll ever be."

Slopitch laughs and looks at me. "Oh, one more thing before we go. I thought I'd let you know that I spoke to the coroner's office a few minutes ago, and they finished a preliminary autopsy report."

"A preliminary autopsy report?" Frankie lets out a laugh of her own. "That's the kind that you do on someone before he's dead, right?"

"No, Mrs. Moony. And I wouldn't be laughing if my husband was in as much trouble as yours could be."

"Oh, I didn't know you were married, Detective Slopitch."

"What?" That one leaves Slopitch scratching his head and gets a small rise out of Clay. As for me, I just stand there beaming at my wife. I'm sure glad she's on my side.

Slopitch's expression turns into a question mark, then he shrugs it off and looks at me. "The coroner says you were right about something, Moony. Dr. Nelson was dosed with"—he pulls a little pad out of his pocket and starts to read—"sodium pentobarbital and a bit of phenytoin sodium." He chuckles as he puts the pad away. "They say that sodium is really bad for your heart. It comes in a product called Euthasol. They use it to put pets to sleep."

I look at Frankie. "The preliminary autopsy report means that the medical examiner read the label on the syringe."

"No, that's not all, wise guy. He noticed deep fingerprint marks on Nelson's arms, which means it was a two-person job—one to hold him down and one to inject him. He also said that whoever injected Dr. Nelson was pretty good with a needle—like a nurse, or a doctor. Or a paramedic."

Slopitch waits for a reaction from me. He gets one from Frankie instead. "Or a fireman or a cop. Some of them have emergency medical training too. Or maybe a seamstress. They're good with needles."

"Uh-huh. Very funny, Mrs. Moony." He turns back to me. "Isn't it a coincidence that there were two of you at Dr. Nelson's office? And one of you is good with a needle. I mean, how many guys does it take to talk to a vet about a cat?"

"Maybe you should be talking to Mrs. Nelson's body-builder boyfriend," I say. "It would take someone really strong to hold someone down, even a small guy like Nelson. Pat Ryan is in his sixties."

"No, I think even a senior citizen like Patrick could have handled it. Nelson had Valium in his system—lots and lots of it. So much that he might have been asleep when they jabbed him. You don't have a prescription for Valium, do you, Moony?"

"No. And it would take a while for the Valium to take effect. I didn't get there until six-thirty. Of course, I didn't get there until after he died. But that doesn't seem to make any difference to you, either."

"What about you, Mrs. Moony? Do you have a prescription for Valium?"

"Maybe. But so do ten million other people."

"I take that as a yes."

"Oh, Jesus." Frankie speaks to Slopitch's partner. "Do you have a prescription for Valium, Miss Clay?"

She shoots a glance at Slopitch before answering. "I'd rather not say."

"Well, I'm sure you could use some after working with this guy all day."

"Very funny." Slopitch lets out a forced laugh. "You want to know something else the ME said, Moony? He said there's not enough of this Euthasol stuff in one syringe to kill a person. It would have taken two shots to do the trick. That's how we know that Dr. Nelson didn't croak himself. And the thing I find interesting talking to you here is that last night you were saying it looked like a suicide, but today you didn't even raise that point when I started questioning you. You knew the doctor wasn't a suicide last night, didn't you?"

"I was trying to save the guy's life, I wasn't trying to solve anything."

"So why aren't you still saying it's suicide today?"

"If it looked like a suicide, would you be here questioning me?"

Slopitch takes a moment to think that one over, but doesn't reply. "So anyway, there was one syringe left on the floor in the back of the office. That leaves one unaccounted for. So, Phil, you wouldn't happen to have one of those syringes around here, would you?"

"If he did, do you think he'd be stupid enough to have it in the house?"

"I don't know, Mrs. Moony, you tell me. How stupid do you have to be to get caught selling drugs outside a Chicago public school?"

Frankie looks like she's about to attack. I hold out my hand as a sign to stay calm. You don't want to give this guy the pleasure of rattling you. And she's been doing so well up to now.

"Buying, not selling," I say. "Half a block from a school. And the charges were dropped. It was in both papers. Maybe you missed it because there weren't any pictures. No, I don't have the goddamn syringe. And I never had it. Any more questions?"

"Nope. Not for now. But if we asked, I suppose you wouldn't mind letting us have a look around."

"Ask and you'll find out."

"Can we have a look around?"

"Without a search warrant? No."

"Oh, a search warrant. You're a lawyer now." He looks at his partner. "Maybe we should go get a search warrant."

"You have to go to a judge to get one," Frankie says.

"Judges are those guys in black robes who preside over courtrooms."

"Thank you, Mrs. Moony. I know some judges."

"I'm sure you do. Some of them are rotten crooks. And my name's not Mrs. Moony."

"Of course not. That's right, you're one of those—"

"One of what?" It's Candy's turn to sound a sour note.

"Oh, brother." Slopitch moves toward the door. "Now I've got two women's libbers mad at me." When he reaches the doorway, he turns. "By the way, Phil. Is that your car parked out front, the LeBaron?"

"Yeah, why?"

"I just noticed that it doesn't have a city sticker on it."

Vehicle stickers are just one of many ways that the city of Chicago likes to shake down its citizens.

Slopitch grins. "You probably want to get one—it would be a shame if you got a ticket." He holds the door for Clay as she walks out. "Pardon my sexism, partner."

She mutters. "Oh, shut up, Dick."

Slopitch treats us to an exit smile. "I sure do love my job."

Twenty-two

Frankie is so angry, she looks like she's about to cry.

"Don't worry," I tell her. "Slopitch is only blowing hot air."

"It's more like noxious fumes. Can you believe the size of the guy's mouth?"

I nod. "I bet he could get a whole doughnut in there, no problem."

"Can that guy really possibly think that you and Pat Ryan killed a vet over a stolen cat?"

"I can't imagine so. I think he just enjoys the harassment part of the job."

"It's probably the only part he does well."

"I don't know. I think we held our own. You especially."

She smiles. "Do you really think so?"

I hold open my arms. "Darling, you were fantastic."

She steps into them and we embrace. "You did good too, Moony," she whispers. "But I still think it would be a good idea to call Burt."

"I don't know. You already know what he's going to say. 'Don't answer any questions without your attorney present.' If you had called him, I'd be down at the police station right now, answering questions with Burt present and the meter running."

"I know. But it's the threat of a search warrant that worries me. You know what they can do to your house. And if he knows the right judge, he can get one on flimsy grounds."

"Okay." I head right for the phone. Given our fragile emotional states after the workout with Slopitch and considering Frankie's hangover, this is one of those things that could turn into a dispute. My response is one of the unwritten rules by which we keep our relationship solid: Avoid the possibility of I-told-you-so's up front.

Fortunately and not surprisingly, Burt is out of the office. Someday I'm really going to need the guy, and I won't feel so lucky. I leave my name and number with an unfamiliar office assistant who could be the new Boogie Woogie Bugle Boy of Burt's firm. Bette Midler is blaring in the foreground.

I call Pat and get Eeny, Meeny, Miney and Mo on the answering machine. I tell them to tell him that Dick Slopitch is on the prowl.

"Well," Frankie says, "what do we do now?"

"We could go visit the folks at We-Mail and see if anyone remembers who sent me that note. Or, after hearing Slopitch's version of what Abby Nelson said, I should probably call her back and press her on a few points."

"Oh, you talked to the merry widow?"

"While you were napping."

"How did she sound?"

"Angry."

"At?"

"The dear departed Edwin. He's left her with a god-awful mess."

"Great. She has the guy killed and then she's pissed at him for dying."

"Hey, you don't know that she killed him. She says she thinks he killed himself."

"Uh-huh. And if you believe that..."

"I didn't say I believed her."

"Okay. But in this case, I'm inclined to believe guilty until proven innocent. Especially if she's filling Slopitch's head with accusations aimed at you."

"She said she thinks Slopitch is out to get me. She suggested a couple of other possible suspects, but he just wanted to know about me."

Frankie's brow furrows. "Maybe you *should* call her."

"Honey, I just don't feel up to it right now. I'd like to talk to Pat first. What do you want to do?"

"I'd like to keep my mind off all this business for a while. I need to clear my head a little."

"There's only one thing that would keep my mind off it."

She smiles and holds out her hands, palms up. "I'm game if you are."

There are some definite advantages to being self-employed and in love with your spouse. Three hours later, we're climbing out of bed and into the darkness of dusk, and I'm telling her how fantastic she is once again. We worked a little nap into the curriculum, so I'm feeling rested as well as energized.

Frankie does a little improvisational dance while improvising dinner, and I've got a little spring in my step while taking out the trash. On my way to the garbage can, I see something that makes me slow down: Melvin Workman, my neighbor from across the alley.

Melvin is a guy who everyone in the neighborhood acts super-nice to, including Frankie and me. And we all do it for the same reason. Melvin and his wife, Sheila, are the only blacks on the block. Hell, they're practically the only blacks on the whole far Northwest Side.

Melvin's a big improvement over his predecessor, Mitch Michaels. He ended up dead in an alley over in Pat's neighborhood, after getting involved in a major-league theft of some baseball cards. But all things considered, I'd have to say that Melvin and Sheila are possibly the most boring couple I've ever known.

For a while, Frankie maintained that the reason they seemed so boring was that all of the neighbors engaged them in boring subjects. But after we had just the two of them to dinner at our house and they had us at theirs, she changed her view.

I hang back at the corner of my garage, but after half a minute I realize it's no use. Melvin has spotted me and is waiting. That's one of his maddening qualities—he waits for you when he sees you. Even among the nicest neighbors and in the nicest neighborhood, there's a tacit understanding that you never wait for anyone out by the trash.

"Tell you what, Phil," Melvin says. "I guess your garbage must be a whole lot more interesting than ours."

"What makes you say that?"

"Because there was a bag lady out here before, right after dinnertime. She gave your garbage a real good going-over, but she didn't even stop to look at mine."

"Is that so?" Out of habit, I answer Melvin without really listening. But three steps closer to my trash can and three steps away from it, his observation suddenly registers. I stop and pay more attention to him than I ever have.

"I was bringing out my first load. On Wednesday night, I always bring out two loads. The first one's from dinner because Sheila likes the dinner garbage to be taken out right away. The second one's all the little wastebaskets from around the house. I pack them all into one of the big trash bags—you know, the thirty-gallon black ones—being Thursday's the day the garbagemen come. I've told you that before, haven't I?"

"Yeah, you have, Melvin."

"Tell you what. It sure beats running out here at eight-thirty in the morning in your bare feet, passing them to the guys while they're busy dumping them."

I don't tell him he's already told me that too. Melvin's story about Frankie running out to catch the trash guys one morning has become neighborhood legend—not because of Frankie's doing it, but because of Melvin's habit of telling it. I've learned there's also no point in explaining to him that she was running out to recover something—a manuscript—not to throw it away.

"What time was that?" I'm still three steps away from my trash can.

"I told you. It was about dinnertime." Leave it to Melvin to give you a precise answer.

"What did she look like?" I'm trying to sound less curious than I usually do about anything Melvin tells me, but that's a tough assignment. Especially because I'm damn curious.

"It wasn't what she looked like. It was what she smelled like that caught my eye. She had on a trench coat that smelled like cat business."

"I see." For some reason, I flash on Millicent Melrose as I move again toward my garbage can. I'm afraid I already know what I'm going to find when I open it, and I'm more afraid of Melvin seeing me find it. I try to convince myself that it was probably just a bag lady who happened to give Melvin's trash a pass.

"Did you see what kind of car she was driving?"

"A car? Phil, I told you, she was a bag lady. Bag ladies don't drive cars. Unless you're from up in Winnetka or somewhere like that."

Winnetka. It would take some work for Abby Nelson to do herself up like a bag lady. But the trench coat that reeks of cat pee would be a cinch.

"I was just kidding, Melvin."

"Oh, you were." He chuckles. "I get it, Phil. That's pretty funny, a bag lady with a car."

I can barely stand the suspense of waiting for Melvin to leave before I look in my trash can. I can't stand the idea of standing there listening to Melvin laugh. And I know from experience that as long as Melvin's laughing, he ain't leaving.

I take a deep breath as I flip back the lid on the can and casually heft my trash bag over the side lip.

It's there. Just as I thought, just as I feared. Nestled between two white trash bags and propped from below by a short stack of *Tribunes* and *Sun-Times*. It may not be the same vial of Euthasol that was used to kill Edwin Nelson, but if the cops find it in my trash, I'll be in jail before I can prove that it wasn't.

My first impulse is to throw my bag down hard on top of it and crush it to pieces. But that might not work, and it would only make it harder to remove later. I know right away that I have to remove it, and I feel an urgent need to make later come as soon as possible. Which means I have to lose Melvin right away. That's easier said than done without running the risk of being rude.

Given the circumstances, that's a risk I'm willing to take. I flip the lid closed, turn and give Melvin a perfunctory wave as I start back toward my walk. "See you later, Melvin. Say hi to Sheila."

"Yeah, sure, okay, Phil, see you later. I guess you must be busy, huh?"

"Yeah, I am, very." As I head up the walk toward the house, I can feel Melvin's gaze following me. I'm on my back steps by the time he turns slowly away and ambles back to his house. I wait until I hear the back door to his house shut, then head straight for my garage.

My heart is racing as I fumble for a pair of work gloves. Whoever the bag lady was who left the syringe in my trash has probably called the cops by now. If it was Abby Nelson, she'd know to ask for Slopitch, so he may be on his way here already. Unless the bag lady was Slopitch's partner, in which case the cops could already be watching.

Despite my sense of paranoia, I don't think that's too likely. It's one thing to come bust my chops, quite another to frame me for a murder. As I slip back out to the alley, my money's on Abby Nelson. And I know this sounds crazy, but amid all my fear and anger, there's a little part of me that has just enough room to feel betrayed. All that sweet talk from Abby has made me a little soft on her.

I take a glance up and down the alley to make sure no one's watching. If someone is, he's well hidden. I walk straight to the trash can, flip the lid up with my left hand, snag the syringe with my right and let the lid drop. I don't allow myself a look around as I go back up the walk to the house. When I reach the steps, I decide there's no way I'm taking the thing inside. I put it behind one of wooden posts for the porch and cover it with leaves.

"I guess you must have run into Melvin," Frankie says, as I enter the kitchen. Her voice is cheerful, but that's about to change.

"Yeah, and it's a good thing I did."

"Why?"

"He told me about a bag lady picking through our trash."

"Such excitement. I'm surprised you were able to get away from him so quickly."

"It took some doing. I was downright rude."

"I doubt he noticed."

"Oh, no, he noticed, but it had to be done. The bag lady didn't take anything from our trash. She put something in there."

"Don't tell me. A syringe?"

I nod. "Give the lady a prize."

"I can do without the prize. Where is it now?"

"I hid it under the back porch. But it won't be there long."

"What are you going to do with it?"

"I'm not sure," I say, as I reach for the phone. "Have you got any ideas?"

"Who are you calling—Pat?"

I nod as I wait through the chorus of meows on his answering machine. This time I don't make any clever remarks. My message is clear and to the point. "Pat, it's Phil. Call me, it's urgent."

Frankie lets out a deep breath as I hang up. "I think we should leave it in the alley behind Purr & Bark. There's probably a Dumpster."

I manage to smile. "Great minds think alike. I'll be back in fifteen minutes."

"I'm coming with you."

"No, I think you should stay here, in case the cops come with a search warrant."

"If the cops come with a search warrant, I don't want to be here."

"Of course you don't. But—"

"Okay, I get it, you're right. One of us has to stay here and watch them."

"Exactly." I open our utility drawer and take out a small brown bag. "Fifteen minutes, promise," I say as I step toward the back door.

"Phil."

I turn. "I know, be careful."

"No, something else." She steps toward me. "I love you."

"Then everything will be just fine."

Twenty-three

It happens two blocks from my house. After taking a left at the corner near Independence Park, I glance in my rearview mirror and see the blue light flashing behind me. It happens so quickly, I think he must be after someone else, but I can see that mine's the only car in sight.

My heart stops before I can stop my car. And I feel some discomfort in my chest that makes me think I better go get checked by a cardio guy. If I live through what's coming next.

I snatch the brown paper bag on the passenger seat and stash it under mine. Then I reach for the glove compartment and grab the state registration certificate and insurance card. Fortunately, we're organized on that score. I can thank Frankie for that, and I do.

By the time he gets to my car, I've got my window rolled down and I'm ready with all the documentation I've got. Which isn't enough. As Slopitch so thoughtfully pointed out earlier, I'm short one city sticker.

"Driver's license and insurance card." He barks, the sound of a very large dog, but to my ears at this moment, it's as comforting as a Mozart concerto. If the cops had been tipped off about the syringe, he would have ordered me out of the car. This has all the markings of a routine harassment stop, courtesy of one large-mouth detective.

I hand him both cards, and the state registration, which he flings right back at me.

"What's the matter, buddy? Can't you follow instructions?"

My heart is no longer in my throat, so I'm tempted to lunge for his. I'd like to ask how long he's been waiting for me, how it feels to be Dick Slopitch's peon, whether he doesn't have anything better to do. But I know better than that. Even an old dog like me can learn a new trick now and then. I bite my tongue and manage to spit out a really bad-tasting response. "I'm sorry, Officer."

He ignores me and begins circling the car, conducting a methodical inspection. It takes about three minutes for him to complete the circuit. When he returns with his findings, I note that he isn't wearing his badge. That's because he doesn't want me to be able to find out who he is. But I've got a surprise for him, even though I may not use it. I remember this bozo from a car-accident call that we both answered a few years ago. I always make it a point to memorize cops' names. His is Joseph Carmody.

"Mr. Moony, you're probably wondering why I stopped you."

"Yes, sir, I am." I'm not, of course, but I'm also not dumb enough to tell the truth.

"Your right taillight is out, did you know that?"

"No, sir, I didn't. Thank you for telling me."

"You also don't have a current city sticker."

"Yes, Officer."

"Are you challenging me? Are you saying you *do* have a city sticker?"

"No, Officer, I'm not. I forgot to get one."

"I see. So you're a forgetful guy. Like I noticed you forgot to put on your seat belt."

This is false and he knows it. Instead of protesting, I look down at my fastened belt and back up at him.

"Oh, sure, it's buckled now. But you did that after I pulled you over. I saw you. Right?"

"Sir, you might have seen me reaching for the glove compartment to get my insurance card."

"You're not calling me a liar, are you?"

"No, sir, I'm not."

"You better not be." He stares, waiting for a response, but I'm done giving responses. "Okay, Moony, you're in some trouble here. I've got to issue a ticket for failure to operate a safe vehicle, failure to display a city vehicle sticker and failure to wear a seat belt. You sound like a real failure."

He chuckles, trying to force a reaction, but I just stare straight ahead.

"And then, of course, you don't have your insurance card."

That does draw a reaction. My head swivels so fast that I may need to file a claim for whiplash.

"Hmmm." He scratches the stubble on his chin. "I know you said you gave it to me, but I can't find it. Do you think it could have blown away?"

If it weren't for the syringe under my seat, I'd be reading this guy the riot act. I'm tempted to let him know I know who he is. Instead, I take two deep breaths. "I don't know, Officer."

"So how do you want to handle this?"

"Excuse me, Officer?" I'm pleading ignorance, but I know what he means, and he knows I know. He's shaking me down for a bribe. It's one of Chicago's most storied traditions, though not as prevalent as it once was. In a normal situation, a twenty-dollar bill would more than take care of things. But this ain't a normal situation. Depending on how far he plans to go to satisfy Dick Slopitch, he could be attempting to trick me into offering a bribe. That's a chance I am not going to take.

He shakes his head in disgust. "I said, 'How do you want to handle this?' You need to post bond. You don't want to have to follow me down to the police station, do you?"

He's failed to mention that I could also let him keep my driver's license or give him a bail-bond card. Now I'm almost certain that he's in this for his own financial interest. There's still an opening for me to offer a bribe without really offering one. I've used it before. In my most naive tone of voice, I could ask if it's possible to pay my bond directly to him. But I'm not going to risk that one, either.

"No, sir, I don't want to go to the station." I take out my wallet and begin flipping slowly through my bills. I stop when I come to my automobile-club card. I can thank Frankie once again that I have one of those. "I'll give you my bond card."

He puffs up his cheeks, forces out a long, irritated sigh and snatches the card from my hand. He starts back toward his car, then stops, turns and treats me to a big smile. "These things have been known to blow away, too." He holds the card by its corner with his thumb and index finger.

"I'm sure they have, Officer."

"Oh, a damn smart-ass. Are you saying the police department is corrupt?"

"No, sir."

"Have you been drinking, Moony?"

"No, Officer, I haven't."

He takes two steps back and switches on his flashlight. "Get out of the car, right now."

I do it very slowly, but I quickly close the door behind me. This is my moment. I stare right at him. "Yes, Officer Carmody."

"What did you call me?" He's aiming the flash right in my eyes. That's no pleasure, but I'd rather it be there than under my seat.

"Officer Joseph Carmody."

He takes the flash off my face, but I'm still blind and vulnerable. Depending on how dumb or mean he is, it could be coming for my head.

Fortunately for me, he's smarter than he is mean. "Back in the car, Moony."

With my pupils shriveled like raisins, I have to feel my way back in. As I sit down, I feel my license bounce across my lap.

"Get the fuck out of here right now, Moony. If you say a word about this to anyone, I'm coming after you and I'm not taking any fucking prisoners. Are we clear on that?"

"Yes, Officer Carmody."

My vision is not what you'd call road-ready, but I take off before he gets back to his car. I turn north on Springfield, west on Dakin, north on Pulaski, west on Irving Park Road. Zig and zag to the Kennedy ramp, before he decides to change his mind.

By the time I hit the Lawrence Avenue exit, my mind has returned to the manageable worry level that it was when I left my house. Which means I still feel like I could wet my pants any moment.

I consider calling Frankie on the cell phone, but I'd only freak her out. Besides, I need my full concentration on the task before me.

As I cross Milwaukee Avenue, I wonder if I should drop the syringe on my initial run through or scout the location first. PURR & BARK is a block west of the post office, so it's not unusual for cars to cruise the side streets and alleys while setting up for a mail drop. This means I won't arouse suspicion. It also means I may encounter some traffic. After careful deliberation, I decide to play it the way I know best—by ear.

To get the best angle on the Dumpster behind the vet's office, I have to take a left off Lawrence. This puts the back wall of the place on my side of the car.

The coast is clear ahead of me when I make the turn. I

slow to a crawl and check my mirror while feeling under my seat for the syringe. Fortunately, Frankie and I did our annual fall cleanup during our road trip to Wisconsin, so I'm able to find the paper bag without having to step on the brake pedal.

With my window rolled down I'm able to toss the bag under the Dumpster, no sweat. As I begin to accelerate, I realize that I'm drenched with sweat. Halfway down the alley, I suddenly feel another round of it coming on. That's when it occurs to me that I've probably left my fingerprints on the bag.

Duh.

I'm too far away to stop and back up. And I'm too far gone even to try to think logically about what I should do next. I take a right at the first corner, a right at the second, a right on Lawrence and a right at the alley. Four rights and I'm right back at the Dumpster. This time I've got to get out of the car. And I'm not thinking about issues of finesse. All I'm thinking is speed.

I get down on my knees and reach under the big green trash bin with my hands. I open the top of the bag, let the syringe slide out, jump back into the car butt-first and I'm out of there. Just as I reach the end of the alley, I see another car turning in from Lawrence. It's too far back for me to be concerned, but when I hit the corner, I'm ready to scoot just the same.

The driver of the mail truck coming from my left has different plans. He's also got his own set of problems.

It's one of those big rigs, half a block long, half a dozen sets of wheels, and an American eagle half the size of Canada perched on the side. One set of the wheels is hung up on the curb, leaving me hung up at the corner, with the eagle's eye trained right on me. Mine is trained on the rearview mirror.

As the headlights behind me get closer, I can make out the form of a roof rack on the approaching car. It's either a cab or a cop. My heart is hoping cab, but my head is betting cop.

Yup, it's a cop. On a night like this, to a guy like me, what else could it be? There are two of them, both of the white-male variety. Luckily, they seem distracted at the moment. A good doughnut can have that effect.

I take my eyes off the mirror to get an update on the truck driver's progress. The news is good and bad. He's got four wheels up on the curb now, but there's probably enough room for me to squeeze by. That would mean cutting him off, or at least the cops might see it that way. I decide to stay put.

Back in my rearview, I can no longer see doughnuts. I can't even see the cops. That's because their dome is flashing. It's another blue-light special, and I'm the one being marked down.

Or so I think. One of the cops clarifies the situation by addressing me through their loud speaker: "MOVE YOUR DAMN CAR, BUDDY."

The noise alone is enough to stop your heart. I can barely find the strength to work the steering wheel, as I maneuver around the truck. The cops barge right past it and continue on by me. The one on the passenger side gives me a wave. I can't tell if it's a friendly or unfriendly gesture, and I don't care one bit.

My foot is shaking so much that I can't keep it steady on the accelerator. I putt-putt all the way up the block back to Lawrence. As I head toward the Kennedy, every tavern light and Old Style sign beckon me to pull over and pull up a stool.

But right now there's only one place I want to be—home, with my wife, and my cat. And I'm more than willing to settle for two out of three.

Twenty-four

Here he is. Oh, he's swerving to the liquor cabinet." Frankie covers the mouthpiece of the phone with her hand and speaks to me. "It's Pat. I've told him about our day."

"You don't know the half of it," I say, as I take the receiver and a gulp of bourbon. That gives her reason to stand there and observe my phone conversation. I'm still so shaky that I can't start to talk about it right away. Instead I inquire about Pat's visit to the nursing home.

"It was great, I took your advice," he says. "I took along a deck of cards. Joe Carney can't walk for shit, but he's still sharp as a tack. I've never been so happy to lose money in my life. He took me for forty-eight bucks. I'm going to call a couple of the other old-timers and we're going to have a poker game there every week. I stayed through dinner. And you know what? The chow isn't so bad."

"Does that mean you're changing your instructions to me?"

"Nah, I wouldn't want to live there. You can still shoot me."

"Were you able to pick up Millicent's cat?"

"Oh, yeah, that went fine too. She's a sweet gal. Made me another cup of tea."

"Did you talk to Madge about the door being locked?"

"Yeah, I did. She says it wasn't, that it just gets stuck."

"I noticed that when I went in."

"Millicent insists it was locked, but Madge says that lady Edith from the White Hen brought over Nelson's tea and Tums, and she was able to get in. Ask again, and each of them will say the same thing. You're not going to change those ladies' minds."

"What about the doorbell. They didn't hear it?"

"Madge says you can't hear the doorbell if you're in the backroom. That's why they leave the front door unlocked. There's a buzzer back there rigged to go off when the door opens.

"She was going nuts over at Nelson's office today. She was running the whole show by herself. Nelson's crazy wife was too depressed to come in, said close up, screw the customers, who gives two turds about their pets. Madge couldn't do that. The phone was ringing off the hook, she was turning customers away. And she had Slopitch there asking questions."

"Yeah, I know. Slopitch said she described me as angry and threatening."

"Well, that's not how she tells it. She says he was pressing her really hard about both of us."

"I talked to Abby this afternoon. She said the same thing."

"What? Did she call you?"

"No, I called her."

"Why did you do that?"

"To offer condolences, I guess. I was the last person to see her husband alive. Plus I was curious to see what she had to say."

"Oh, come on." Frankie pokes me in the ribs. "You were curious to find out if she still had that cat hanging on her rack."

"Excuse me, Pat." I hold up a finger at Frankie. "Honey, this is serious. If you—"

"Yeah, yeah, I know. I'll cut the commentary. But when are you going to tell him about what just happened? I don't need to hear about your conversation with the Wide-Load-Widow again."

"I'm getting to that."

"Well, I'll get you dinner while you're getting there. Just make sure you let me know when you get there, okay?"

"Promise." I take my hand off the mouthpiece. "So, Pat, where was I?"

"You were—" It takes me a moment to realize he's laughing. "You were talking to the Wide-Load Widow." As his laugh dies out, it's strangled by a cough. "You are one lucky guy, Phil."

"I'm not feeling so lucky today."

"But you married lucky, that's the important part. Unlike Dr. Nelson. So, anyway, the widow was saying . . ."

"She said that Slopitch seemed to have it in for me. And for you."

"Well, he hasn't gotten to me yet, so I'm going to him first thing in the morning. And he's not going to like the way I do it. I'm going to go to Dan Hynes, he's the head of Area Five. That should put an end to this nonsense."

"Slopitch said you don't have any friends left down there."

"He's full of it. But Dan Hynes isn't exactly a friend. He's just a reasonable guy and a very good cop. There are a lot of them, you know."

"I'll take your word for it."

"That crap Slopitch pulled on you at your house today, he can't get away with that."

"It gets worse."

"You mean the surprise you found in your trash-can? Frankie told me about that. As much of a jerk as the guy is, I seriously doubt that he planted it."

171

"No, I don't think he planted it. I think that's the work of a phony bag lady with a Winnetka address."

"AKA—"

"The Wide-Load Widow, yes."

"I'm inclined to think that too. Except for something Madge told me today. Now remember, she has nothing nice to say about Nelson's wife. But she doesn't think Abby could have killed him. She says that despite all her nagging, Abby really needed the guy."

"You might tell Hynes that one of Nelson's customers threatened to kill him last year. Abby told me that. Apparently, the guy's cat died."

"No, it was the guy's girlfriend's cat. Madge told me about him. She's pretty sure the guy's on the fire department. Does the name Zachary Taylor ring any bells for you?"

"Zachary Taylor. That sounds familiar. What does he look like?"

"She doesn't know. She never saw him. Evidently, the guy kept calling Nelson on the phone and threatening him. She said he was really shaken up. She told him to go to the police, but he wouldn't. After what Frankie found out about the guy's history, I think we know why. And here's the part that should interest you. She said Nelson finally got the guy to lay off by enlisting the help of another one of their customers—your pal Ron Ostrow."

"Really. So this Taylor is a friend of Ostrow's."

"Apparently. Or at least they know each other from working together. That part's not clear. Madge thinks Ostrow may have been the guy who recommended Nelson to them in the first place. And something else."

"What's that?"

"Madge thinks Nelson paid them off. Ostrow came in to see him one evening right after they closed up. She overheard them talking about Taylor, and then Ostrow left with an envelope. After that, no more calls."

I move into the kitchen and consult Frankie. "Do we know someone named Zachary Taylor?"

She nods. "He was the twelfth President of the United States. Old Rough and Ready. He built his popularity by slaughtering Indians. He died in office after about a year. Dinner's ready." She points to a mountain of spaghetti on the table.

"Taylor was a President," I tell Pat.

"What? Of the union?"

"No, of the country."

"I don't think we're talking about the same guy."

"Nope, I guess not. Even if that's all true—Ostrow, Taylor, Taylor's girlfriend—who would have known about me to leave the syringe in my Trash can?"

"Now that's a very good question. And another one that I hope to get an answer to tomorrow. Did everything go okay getting rid of that thing?"

"Not exactly."

"Tell me what happened."

I motion to Frankie. "We're getting there."

It's a long wait for the two of them, being I'm eating spaghetti while telling the story. It takes a lot to get Pat mad, but by the time I finish relating the whole sordid tale of my encounter with Officer Joseph Carmody, he sounds furious.

"Goddammit! That settles it. I'm calling Hynes at home right now."

Pat's voice is so loud, I have to hold the phone away from my ear. Frankie's ranting even louder about calling Charlotte Penske. With both of them yelling, it's a wonder I'm able to hear the beep on the line telling me I've got another call.

I ask Pat to hold on, but I'm not sure he hears me. My other caller is far more sedate, but he's excited in his own way.

"Phil, this is Melvin." The guy only lives across the alley, but it takes me a moment to place him outside of that context. By that time, he's already filling it in for me. "Melvin Workman, your neighbor from across the alley?"

"Sure, hello, Melvin. Listen, I'm on another call right now, can I call you back?"

"Sure, but me and Sheila are about to go to bed, and this will only take a moment, and it might be important, so—"

"Okay, Melvin, what is it?"

"So I guess you must have call-waiting too. I'd like to talk to you sometime about how you like it. The jury's still out on it for me. It's good if you have an important call or something. But when you're trying to have a conversation with someone and then somebody calls and it's not important, it can be really aggravating, if you know what I mean."

"Yeah, I know what you mean, Melvin. And you're calling because . . . ?"

"Oh, right. Well, Sheila didn't think I should call so late, but I figured you'd want to know."

"Want to know what, Melvin?"

"Remember I told you about that bag lady looking through your garbage earlier? Well, you're not going to believe this, but Sheila was looking out the kitchen window a few minutes ago, and all of a sudden, she says, 'That's strange.' So I say, 'What's strange, honey?' And she says, 'You're not going believe it if I tell you, so you better come see for yourself.' So I did and you know what?"

"No, Melvin, tell me, please."

"First it was the bag lady, now it's the police out there going through your trash."

"When?" I'm already walking to the back door.

"Now. They're still out there. Isn't that—"

"Thanks, Melvin, I really appreciate you calling."

"Jesus." Frankie's next to me at the door. "Is that the police out there?"

"I'm afraid so." I click to the other line. Pat is no longer on the line. I click off and dial his number.

"What happened?" he asks. "Did we get cut off?"

I could tell Pat about my call from Melvin, but I'm afraid he might want to weigh in on the merits of call-waiting himself. "Yeah, we got cut off," I say. "And Slopitch is out in the alley searching through my trash can."

"Does he have a search warrant?"

"I don't know. He didn't announce himself. I don't think he knows we know he's out there."

"I'll be right over. Try not to let him in, but if he's got a warrant, you've got to."

Twenty-five

From the darkened kitchen, we have an obstructed view of the alley. I think there are six of them—Slopitch, Candy Clay, and four uniforms.

Actually, there are eight, if you include the two bathrobes. Melvin and Sheila are the center of attention.

"Well," says Frankie, "at least that should buy us a little time."

Not much. In less than a minute, five of them file inside our gate and start to fan out over the lawn with flashlights. We don't have a large backyard. They're practically bumping into each other. Slopitch doesn't have a light. He's busy keeping his arms folded and his mouth moving. Only Candy remains in the alley, still listening to Melvin.

Frankie sighs. "Looks like old Melvin has bored them right out of the alley."

"Do you think he told them I'm home?"

"I doubt they let him get that far."

Two of the uniforms go to the garage. The others move toward the house, shining their lights under the porch.

"Oh, I hope one of them steps on a fucking rake." Frankie

strides away from the window long enough to grab her glass of wine off the table.

"Why just one of them?"

"The others I want to step on rusty nails."

"I hope our liability insurance is paid up."

"It's paid up, don't worry."

"Then I hope Slopitch falls right through the porch."

"I swear, if they come in here and any of them . . ." Frankie's voice starts to crack, and I realize she's fighting back tears. I reach out and squeeze her hand. "If any of them damages anything, I swear I'll . . ."

"Sue their asses. You always sue their asses."

She forces a smile. "That's right. You sue their asses, grab their assets."

"This is all going to turn out okay. It's just going to be a little bit unpleasant."

"I know."

They're all moving toward the porch now, even Candy. This leaves Melvin and Sheila out in the alley, but they're not alone. Hank Gregor, their neighbor to the south, is probably regretting that he picked this moment to take out his trash.

Once the cops are on the porch, we can't see them. Unless we move to the door. We're not going to do that until they knock. And we may just let them knock a few times before we do.

It seems like it's taking a long time for them to get around to it. Maybe something on the porch has attracted their attention. Or maybe my dread is making it seem longer than it is. Whatever the case, I'm so focused on the back door that the pounding on the front makes me jump out of my socks.

"I guess they've decided to come in the front way," Frankie says.

She's wrong, and sometimes that's a good thing. Like now, when I open the door to find friend instead of foe. I'm always glad to see Pat Ryan, but I've never been so happy to see him as I am now.

He bursts right through the doorway and heads for the kitchen. He's waving a cell phone. "I spoke to Dan Hynes on the way over here. You've got nothing to worry about."

From the back porch comes the unmistakable voice of Dick Slopitch. "Phillip Moony, open up. Chicago police. We have a warrant to search the premises."

"Allow me to do the honors," Pat says. He opens the door with a grand, sweeping gesture. "Good evening, Detective Slopitch, we've been expecting you."

"Well, well, surprise, surprise." The smirk on Slopitch's face is so wide that it can barely fit through the door. "Patrick, what are you doing here?"

Pat holds out his hand, and it's not to shake. "May I see the warrant, please?"

"Why, soitanly."

Pat speaks to us without looking up. "On election day, remember to pay your disrepects to Judge Nicholas Kilger."

One of Chicago's more charming political oddities is that judges are voted into office, just like adlderman and sewer commissioners. Every two years, they come up for retention. In your average patronage-infested swamp, you'd expect judges to be appointed by the powers-that-be. But Chicago is special. Here the pols in the Democratic Party who run the city know they have the political muscle to put anyone they want into black robes. And no one can accuse them of appointing their pals.

"Nick Kilger! He made judge?" Frankie looks at me. "C-student from the state's attorney's office." She looks at Slopitch. "What is he—your cousin?"

The detective could not control his grin if he wanted to. "On my mother's side." He snatches the paper from Pat's hand.

As Frankie reaches out to take it from him, Pat holds up his telephone. "Before your guys begin, Dick, I have an important phone call for you." He presses the redial button, then hands the phone to Slopitch. "Commander Hynes for you, Detective."

"What is this?" The glow on Slopitch's face wanes a bit as he puts the phone to his ear. "Commander Hynes, this is Detective Slopitch. Yes, sir, yes, sir. But sir, I have a warrant. We got a tip from a lady who saw the syringe in Moony's garbage can. Yes, sir, we did. No, sir, it wasn't, but . . . Yes, sir, I know, sir, but . . . Yes, sir, yes, sir."

Slopitch hands the phone back to Pat. He looks like he'd like to throw it.

"Well, Detective Slopitch, it sounds like you really told him a thing or two." Being gracious in victory is not Frankie's strong suit.

"Lady, you've got a mouth on you that I don't like."

"Oh dear, how will I ever get over the pain of that?"

With Frankie and Slopitch in a stare-down, Pat picks up the conversational slack. "Dick, did it occur to you that the person who phoned in your tip about a syringe would also be the person who planted the syringe and very likely the person who committed the murder?"

"Of course it did. But it's not there now, which means that Moony must've have taken it." He looks at me. "So what did you do with it?"

"Nothing. I don't know anything about it. I never saw it. My neighbor tells me there was a bag lady out there looking in my garbage can earlier. I guess she took it."

"Or maybe it was never there in the first place," Frankie says. "Maybe I'm the one who phoned in the tip."

The detective is not the only one baffled by that remark. Pat's forehead wrinkles like a raisin, and I'm sure my expression is just as puzzled.

"And just why in the world would you do that?" Slopitch asks.

"Maybe I liked the idea of you having to waste your time picking and sniffing through our garbage like a rat."

"Lady, I've still got a warrant, and I'm going to talk to the commander tomorrow, and there's a real good chance I'll be coming back. And when I do, I'm going to start right in your underwear drawer."

"Whatever gets you off, Detective."

"Hey, that's enough." Clay steps in front of her partner and puts up her hand.

Pat is right behind her. "Yeah, more than enough."

Slopitch wheels and stomps out the back door. The four uniformed cops, all looking a bit sheepish, follow like sheep. Trailing behind them, a red-faced Clay offers a parting thought. "Getting him all riled up really doesn't do any good, you know."

"Then try riling his fat ass down," Frankie says, moving quickly to close the door and almost bumping Clay's butt with it as she does.

Pat accepts Frankie's invitation to stay for a glass of wine, and is also persuaded to partake of an eleventh-hour meal. Between bites, he dishes out some advice on being less confrontational with cops, but she doesn't have much of an appetite for that right now. He also advises getting a good night's sleep, but even that idea doesn't settle too well with her. She claims to be too worked up even to think about it.

Me, I've got no problem thinking about it or doing it—I leave them squabbling at the kitchen table. When I wake up eight hours later, I feel like a million bucks. Well, okay, maybe only a million *lire*. There's a cup of hot coffee on my nightstand and a *Sun-Times* on the bed. After a couple of breaths, I even detect the aroma of bacon wafting up from the kitchen. Frankie is going all out, and while I know her to be thoughtful, devoted, generous and just generally wonderful, I feel the need for pause.

I find good reason for it on page two. That's where Charlotte Penske's column appears.

I don't make the top of the column. That's reserved for

the Mayor's wife, who is spearheading another charitable initiative that will probably garner her husband a few thousand more votes and a few hundred thousand more in campaign contributions, none of which he really needs. My little story runs at the bottom, where Charlotte usually posts birthday greetings to our town's biggest movers and shakers. I wonder if any of them will hold it against me personally that they got bumped.

Here's what it says:

> You come across a dying man and try to save his life. That makes you a Good Samaritan, right? Wrong! Not if you're Phil Mooney, the former paramedic ousted from the fire department for his political support of Mayor Harold. With no evidence against him except his heroic efforts to save Dr. Edwin Nelson, Mooney has been targeted by a certain overweight Area 5 detective investigating the death of the Northwest Side vet. Bad enough that said detective darkened Mooney's doorstep, leveled unfounded accusations and made disparaging remarks to his wife (former *Sun-Times* whiz Frankie Martin). But was it really necessary to keep a patrol car parked outside their house and have a cop stop Mooney for imaginary traffic violations the instant he got in his car? Dear Detective D. S. and Officer J. C.: Are you guys familiar with the term "harassment"?

Frankie smiles as I enter the kitchen with the paper under my arm. "*Buon giorno, carissimo mio.* Pancakes, eggs, bacon."

I pour myself more coffee, sit down at our breakfast nook and read the short item in the local news roundup under the headline POLICE SUSPECT FOUL PLAY IN VET'S DEATH. There's no mention of Pat or me, just an identification of

Nelson and a comment from police that forensic evidence indicates he might not have committed suicide, as first suspected.

"Are you going to speak to me sometime today?" she asks.

"I guess I know who you called after I went to bed last night."

"I thought we should do something, Phil. And you'll notice that I didn't tell her anything about the syringe."

"I figured she was saving that part for tomorrow's paper."

Frankie steps behind me and rubs my shoulders. "It's a good item, don't you think?"

"It could have been better."

That puts a sudden end to my massage. "How?" Frankie's taking offense here because she knows I know that she wrote the item. Charlotte gets great scoops, but if it's longer than a sentence, you have to help her a little.

"The next time you dictate an item to Charlotte, maybe you should spell out my name for her."

"I know. I did. But she still got it wrong. Is that all you have to say?"

I shake my head. "Delicious breakfast, darling."

Twenty-six

Thanks to Charlotte Penske, I'm having one of those mornings when call-waiting seems like either a very good or a very bad thing. If I had time, I could call Melvin and chew it over.

The first call is from Burt Levison, who wants to know why I don't call my attorney before I call my gossip columnist. I tell him that I'm not responsible for the item and that I did the responsible thing and called him.

"I didn't get any message."

"I left one."

"Don't lie to your lawyer, Phil."

"Burt, I don't even lie to gossip columnists anymore. I spoke to a guy yesterday who—"

"Oh, here it is. It was under one of my briefs."

"The jockeys or the boxers?"

"Phil, that's the oldest joke in the lawyer book."

"No, it's not. What about the difference between the dead lawyer and the dead rat in the road?"

"Yeah, I know, skid marks in front of the rat. I know what happened with your message." He lowers his voice. "We've got this gay guy working here as an intern."

"What does being gay have to do with it? How would you like it if someone criticized one of your secretaries because she was a Jewish American Princess?"

"A Jewish American Princess would be fine. Her I could relate to. This guy, there's something very strange about him. He's number five in his class at Northwestern."

"What's wrong with that?"

"Nothing. But why isn't he working at a good firm?"

"Maybe he's going undercover for the Attorney Discipline and Registration Commission."

Burt lowers his voice another notch. "Don't joke about that. One of our guys is in very hot water with them."

"Anyone I know?"

"Yeah, the guy who handled your real estate closing."

"Perry Mathers?"

"Yeah, Perry. It seems he double-billed a few clients."

"How many is a few?"

"Oh, a few hundred. Nothing to shout about." Burt raises his voice to normal level, which is close to a shout. But he sounds far away, which means he's switched to his speakerphone. It's also my tipoff that we shouldn't discuss Perry's predicament any further.

"Okay, Phil, fill me in. I'll buy you breakfast." This means Burt will listen to my tale while he eats his bagel. If it were a face-to-face, he'd split it with me. As usual, he proves to be everything you need in a lawyer—a guy who can give you a good earful even while he's got a mouthful. Within five minutes, he's exacted half a dozen promises about not saying anything to anybody without checking with him first. He says the judge who issued the warrant is a Machine hack from the First Ward. When I tell him about the syringe, I think I might have to perform the Heimlich maneuver telephonically.

"Burt, are you still there?"

"Yeah, I'm here, Phil.

That's when my first call-waiting beep comes. I think

about ignoring it. After all, Burt's a lawyer. But then I realize that the only thing I'm keeping him from is his bagel. I ask him to hold.

It's my ex, Kadie Thurmond, making good on her threat to call about lunch.

"Kadie, can I call you back? I'm talking to my lawyer."

"After seeing this thing in the paper, I'm not surprised." She giggles. Which makes me realize how little desire I have to go to lunch with her. I start to tell her I can't make it, but she says she's not calling about that, she needs to talk to me about something else.

Back on the other line, Burt asks where we were.

"The syringe."

"Yeah, that's right. So you know where this thing is and you think you could get your hands on it if you wanted to?"

"Sure, but I don't want to. That would leave fingerprints."

"Very funny. You're taking this all a little too lightly, Phil. This is evidence in a homicide. I'm not comfortable with it. I think we might want to turn the syringe over to the police."

"I'm not at all comfortable with that."

"There's a procedure to do it. I'm going to talk to one of the attorneys here about it and see what he thinks."

"Not Perry, I hope."

"God no. Now if the police return with a search warrant, you call here right away. And you've got my pager number, right?"

Another call-waiting signal beckons, so I tell him I do, even though I don't. After hearing his contemplated course of action, I think I might be better off giving him the dodge.

It's Pat and he sounds pissed, and I think I know why. But I don't bring up the Poison Pen item right away. I want to get his reaction to Burt's idea about picking up the syringe.

"Tell him it's not there anymore," he says.

"Are you saying I should lie to my lawyer?"

"Why not? A lawyer is a guy you pay to lie for you. Why shouldn't you lie to him? Besides, it wouldn't be a lie."

"What do you mean?"

"I stopped by Purr & Bark and picked it up."

"Why did you do that?"

"I want to be able to get my hands on it if we need it."

"You mean in case we need to move it into the proximity of the person who really did kill Nelson?"

"You said that, not me."

"It sounds like you and my lawyer think alike."

"Thanks for the compliment. By the way, do you know the difference between a dead lawyer and a dead rat in—"

"Skid marks. So, where did you put it?"

"I guess you heard that one already. That's something neither you or your lawyer needs to know. When you do, if you do, I'll tell you. You're better off that way, believe me."

I believe him, but I'd still like to know. But I also know better than to ask again. Despite the lawyer joke, he still sounds pissed.

"Well, I guess your little chat with my wife about not being confrontational with the cops really worked, huh?"

"You mean the piece in the paper? Actually, I thought it was a pretty nice little story. It'll keep them on their toes and maybe off yours."

"I thought you'd be mad."

"No, not at all. But I talked to Dan Hynes and he sure is."

"You mean at Slopitch."

"No. At me, at you, at your wife."

"He doesn't even know my wife."

"He knows of her, believe me. He wants me to come down and see him, have a sit-down with Slopitch, answer their questions about Nelson."

"It sounds like you're being called in for questioning."

"That's exactly what it is. Today is my turn, yesterday was yours. And he sounds almost mad enough to give you another one. I'm going to have to talk him out of executing that warrant again."

"Do you want to take my lawyer along with you?"

"If I take along your lawyer, I'll have to take along my toothbrush. I'll be able to handle them just fine. But they are pissed."

"All because of the item in the paper."

"Yeah, mostly."

"But you liked it and you aren't mad at Frankie about it?"

He laughs. "How could I be mad at your wife? Boy, was that pasta good. You are one lucky guy, Phil."

I look at Frankie, who has moved toward me upon hearing her name spoken. "Pat isn't mad at you about the Poison Pen item."

She grins. "Of course he's not. He helped me write it."

Twenty-seven

Pat advises holding off on going to see Dave Zezel again. Despite the Z on his license plate and his overly friendly manner, there's nothing solid to connect him with Phull's disappearance. He also advises me not to do anything dumb, like call Abby Nelson and ask if she put a syringe in my trash.

"I guess I'm just supposed to sit home and wait for Dad to tell me what to do."

"Like I'm supposed to feel sorry for you? Home with that wonderful wife, and you're going to get bored?"

"My wife likes me out of the house during the day, Pat. It's one of the things that helps her stay wonderful."

"Oh, yeah, that makes some sense. Well, there's a couple things you could do. It wouldn't hurt to stop by that We-Mail store and see if they remember who sent you the package. You could also call around to some of your old buddies and find out if they know this Zachary Taylor. I'm going to check if he's with the police department when I'm down with Hynes."

"Are we trying to find my cat or are we trying to find Nelson's killer?"

"Phull comes first. But someone's trying to pin Nelson on us. So let's get ourselves some breathing room. Besides, whoever killed the doc just might have your cat."

"Okay. You'll call me when you're done with the cops?"

"You mean when they're done with me."

"You can handle them. I've got faith in you."

"Yeah, I'll call you. And by the way, there is one more thing you could do."

"What's that?"

"Go to a currency exchange and get yourself a damn city sticker."

"Oh, yeah, right away."

I barely have time to get the receiver down before the next call comes in. It's Van McNulty, my paramedic pal.

"Are you calling me about that beer already? It's a little early in the day for me."

"Yeah, I guess you're right. We must be getting old. I'm finishing up seventy-two hours off and I feel like I need a vacation."

"Seventy-two. That sounds sweet."

"It's nice, Phil, real nice. But you get spoiled quick. You start wondering where your Daley Day is."

When I was on the fire department, paramedics worked twenty-four hours on, forty-eight hours off, just like firemen. Twice a month, you'd get a bonus day off. It was called your Daley Day, after Mayor Daley, who bestowed it on us as a way of cutting back on overtime pay. In 1994, the system changed for EMTs. They had to give up their Daley Day, but they work twenty-four on, seventy-two off. With 24/48, most guys on the fire department have a second occupation. With seventy-two off, you could have a whole other life.

"Van, it doesn't beat what I have—a hundred sixty-eight off, a hundred sixty-eight off."

"Bullshit, you miss it, Moony. I could tell you miss it, the other night."

189

"Yeah, I miss it sometimes. But the other night, I wish I'd missed that altogether."

"Because of the cops, you mean. Yeah, I'll bet you do. This Slopitch is a real bad actor. But I guess you've been able to figure that out for yourself."

"And I guess you saw this morning's paper?"

"Sure did. And it made my day. Not them harassing you, but you hitting them back. I bet he's shitting a brick. I love it, because he's a damn bully. I ran into him once before, there was a shooting near Douglas Park. There's a little kid there who's a cousin of the kid who got shot. He can't be more than ten years old. Now I know about young gang-bangers, I'm not naive. But this kid is totally distraught about his cousin getting shot. And Slopitch comes on to the kid like he's the one who shot him. It was so bad, his partner ends up having to pull him aside and tell him to lay off. It was totally unnecessary. Just like what he's doing to you. So watch out for this guy, he's way out there."

"I know, I'm watching, believe me." I'm tempted to tell him about Slopitch sulking away with his search warrant last night, but my lawyer's admonitions are still fresh in my mind.

"Well, I just wanted to call, make sure you're okay. If there's anything I can do to help, let me know. And let's get that beer."

"Definitely, we'll do that. And maybe there is something you can do."

"What's that?"

"Do you know a guy on the fire department named Zachary Taylor?"

"EMT or fireman?"

"I'm not sure he's either. He could be a cop."

"I don't know, the name sounds familiar."

"He was the twelfth President of the U.S."

"Yeah, that might be who I'm thinking of."

"Would you ask around—see if anyone knows the guy, and let me know what you find out?"

"Sure, why do you want to know?"

"It's too complicated to explain now. I'll tell you the whole story when we get that beer."

"Sounds good. Well, Moony, I'm sorry about your situation, but it's good to know you haven't lost the knack."

"The knack for what?"

"For getting into strange situations. But you sure missed a crazy scene at the hospital the other night."

"Which hospital?"

"Resurrection. When we took in Dr. Nelson. His wife shows up with this cat the size of a raccoon hanging on her chest. You should see this babe sometime. She's got an amazing shelf. And she's wearing this workout suit that's about three sizes too small. Anyway, she wants to bring the cat with her while she sees her husband, but they won't let her. So she flips out. First she's all distraught, sobbing about her husband dying and how can they be so mean. The next minute she's doing the heavy number. Threatens to sue their asses, says she'll have all their jobs if they don't cooperate. I thought she and this nurse were going to come to blows. All the while this cat is just perched up there, taking it all in."

"So what happened?"

"One of the nurses goes and gets the ER director. He and the missus talk for a few moments over in the corner, and he decides to let her in. If you ask me, I think it was her physical attributes that persuaded the guy."

"I've met her. She can be very persuasive. You must have been hanging around there quite some time. What was the holdup?"

"No, we weren't. She got there a few minutes after we did."

"Are you sure about that?"

"Yeah, why? It was seven-thirty exactly. I let young Jason

do the paperwork, and I was out front watching TV. The Blackhawks game was just starting."

"And what time did you leave Nelson's office? It was after seven, wasn't it?"

"Yeah, it had to be. I don't know exactly. Why?"

"It's kind of complicated."

"I know, you'll tell me over the beer, right?"

"Right." I hear a click on the line that's a beep at his end. That's our signal to end the call.

"Now that's odd," I say to Frankie after I hang up.

"What's odd?"

I relate McNulty's tale of Abby in the ER.

She shrugs. "Sounds like normal Abby behavior to me."

"It's not her behavior that's the odd part. It's that she got to the hospital so soon. Remember Slopitch saying how she couldn't have had time to get home from the vet's office?"

Frankie nods. "Call-forwarding."

"What?"

"She has her calls forwarded to her car phone." Frankie picks up our phone and begins to dial.

"You're not calling Abby, are you?"

"Nope. Ameritech." She sits down at the kitchen table and puts her feet up. "This could take a while."

I watch as she presses a series of buttons in response to the recorded prompts. In about five minutes, she's talking to a customer service representative from our local phone company.

"Hello, Lydia, my name's Abby. And I'm so embarrassed. I have probably the dumbest question anyone's ever asked you." She shoots me a big smile. "Oh, you do? Well, that's good to know. Maybe it's not so dumb after all."

Frankie covers the mouthpiece and asks me for a pen. I deliver it with a notepad from a local real estate agent who never tires of mailing out announcements about her membership in the billionaire sales circle.

"Here's my problem. My husband had our call-forwarding

feature set to forward calls from our house to our car. But I accidentally did something to cancel it out, and now I'm trying to reset it, but I can't remember what our car phone number is. And he's away, so I can't ask him. Is there any way you can look it up for me? It's listed under Edwin Nelson in Winnetka."

Frankie raises her eyebrows at me, signaling that she's run into a possible snag. "Yes, that's right, I know. Our cell phone is with a different company. But I don't know the name of it and they're so hard to get through to. But I had a call forwarded to me on Monday night when it was working, so I was hoping maybe you could look up that call and . . ."

Frankie's eyebrows rise again, but this time there's a smile below that's pushing them up. "Oh, you can? That would be great. It was Monday, around seven o'clock."

Frankie recites Nelson's number without hesitation, filling me with awe over her memorization skills. Then I realize that she's reading the number off Abby Nelson's newspaper ad, which she has taped to our refrigerator. I'm still filled with awe, but over her organizational skills and eyesight.

She nods and smiles as she writes on the notepad. "Thank you, Lydia, you've been such a dear. Now my husband won't think I'm a ditz." She laughs. "That's right. We don't want to give them any ammunition, do we? You have a nice day too."

Frankie leaps out of the chair with her hand set to receive a high five. I give her that and a hug.

Looking over my shoulder, she reads from her pad. "Okay, seven-oh-two Monday evening. Call from Nelson's office to Nelson's house to Nelson's cell phone. I'd say that runs circles around Abby Nelson's alibi, wouldn't you?"

"Yes, indeed. I bet it will even make Dick Slopitch's head spin."

Twenty-eight

Well, we've got some great information," Frankie says. "But what are we going to do with it?"

"Why not just call our pal Dick Slopitch and help him out?"

"Over my dead body."

"What's the matter—you don't want to see what he looks like when his head spins?"

"No, thank you."

"You'd be flaunting your superior powers of detection right in his face."

"I don't ever want to have to look at his ugly face again."

"We could call his partner instead. That would probably piss him off."

Frankie's face brightens at that notion. "Yeah, give it to Candy Clay. Great idea." She starts toward the phone, but I put my arm out to stop her.

"Let's wait and talk to Pat before we call the cops. He practically made me swear an oath."

"He didn't make me take any oath."

"Now, Frankie."

She stops. "Yeah, maybe you're right. Maybe I should call Charlotte instead."

Oh, Jesus, here we go. "Pat said to talk to him before we call anyone." That makes her pause, but I don't think it will be for long. "Besides, he'd feel bad if you didn't let him help." That line of appeal seems to take better hold.

The ringing of the phone ends our standoff, at least for the moment.

"You answer it," I say. "It could be Burt. He wants to recover the syringe and turn it over to the police."

"Oh, great idea." She shakes her head and raises her eyes to heaven. What she sees is the peeling paint and fluorescent wonderland of our kitchen ceiling. We've been meaning to fix that since the day we moved in.

"Tell him I'm not home, okay?"

"Don't worry. I'll do better than that."

She doesn't have to. I can tell by her reaction to the caller that our attorney is still busy plotting strategy.

"Yes, can I tell him who's calling?" Her brow furrows as she gets the answer. "Just a moment." She covers the mouthpiece with her hand. "One of your old squeezes. Kadie Thurmond?"

"Oh, yeah." Now it's my turn to glance upstairs. "Is that how she identified herself?"

"No, you did, after you mentioned her in your sleep the other night. Don't you remember?"

Uh-uh, I sure don't. And I sure hope I haven't been dreaming about Abby Nelson.

"She sounds like someone from your blond period."

"Nope. Black hair, darling, just like you."

"Is she the one whose cat you killed that time?"

"That was her girlfriend, Ellyn Miller. And I didn't kill the cat. It just died on me while they were away."

As I put the phone to my ear, Frankie folds her arms and plants her feet, setting up to monitor the proceedings.

"Kadie, I'm sorry I didn't call back. I've been on the phone all morning."

"That's okay. I'll bet it's been ringing off the hook. Everyone wants to talk to the celebrity."

"Yeah, or something like that."

"Phil, I know you probably think I'm calling about going to lunch. But that's not it."

"What? You mean you don't want to go to lunch with me?" I'm eyeing Frankie, who frowns and moves her hands to her hips. Call me a cad, but I like the idea of being able to tease two women with one line.

"No, I wouldn't mind. I was thinking that your wife probably wouldn't be too crazy about the idea."

I could counter that by mentioning what a reasonable person Frankie is, but why ruin a good excuse when you've got one?

"The reason I'm calling is to ask you about your neighborhood. I'm thinking about buying a house, and I've got an appointment with a realtor this afternoon. I wanted to know how you like living up there. I've heard it's pretty nice."

"Well, yeah, it is, I guess."

She giggles. "You don't sound so sure."

"No, I'm really not." What I'm really not sure about is whether I'd want to have Kadie living on my block. Check that. I *am* sure I don't want Kadie living on our block.

"Well, then, why did you move up there?"

"Because Frankie, my wife, inherited the house from her father. It needed to be fixed up before she could sell it, so we decided to move in. Since then, inertia's taken over and we haven't found the energy to move."

"Oh, I see." Her giggle turns into a full-fledged laugh. "Sounds like you're there until you die, Phil."

I look at the kitchen ceiling and resolve to have it fixed by the end of the year. For an instant, I think about asking Kadie if she wants to buy the place. We could skip the realtors and pocket their commissions. Hell, we could leave the kitchen for her to fix. Instead, I give her the straight dope.

"A few things you should know about the Northwest Side, Kadie. If you move here, you won't find a decent restaurant for miles. There are no shops worth going into, unless you're trying to get your vacuum cleaner fixed. Basically it's got all the disadvantages of the suburbs and all the disadvantages of the city. The cultural center of my existence is the twenty-four-hour Dominicks supermarket."

"Wow, you're making it sound really attractive."

"If you're married and have kids, it makes a lot of sense. But for you, even for us, it really doesn't."

Frankie nods, more to affirm the truth of what I'm saying than to encourage this particular avenue of discouragement.

"Well," Kadie says, back to regular giggle level again, "I guess I can scratch one more neighborhood off my list. Ellyn's the one who's hot on me moving up there. That's probably because she's so bored. Oh, by the way, Phil: Ellyn told me to tell you that she finally forgives you for killing her cat."

"Well, that's awfully big of her, being I didn't actually do anything to her cat."

"Oh, come on, Phil, I think that was just her way of saying there are no hard feelings."

"Ellyn always did have a way with words. When did she tell you that anyway?"

"Remember last week, when I saw you outside your vet's office? I was going to Ellyn's house. She was having a birthday party for this new guy she's seeing. Zack the cop. I told you that. Remember?"

"Oh, yeah, that's right."

"Uh-oh, not you too."

"Not me too what?"

"Alzheimer's. You used to have the best memory of anyone I know."

"Well, we've all got to lose it sometime." I don't see any point in telling her that my memory's as good as ever, it's just that I immediately delete any info that I have no interest in. And there's almost no subject I'd be less interested in than Ellyn Miller and her new boyfriend. Unless . . .

"The guy's name is Zack and he's a cop?"

"Yeah, well, no. His name's Zack, but he's not a cop. I just thought he was. It turns out he's a fireman. The last guy she was dating was a cop." She giggles. "I think she's working her way down the ladder, if you know what I mean."

"Yeah, sure. Pretty soon, she'll be going with a guy from Streets and San."

"Oh, I didn't mean any offense to you, Phil. Paramedics are different."

"Of course. Kadie, does this Zack have a last name?"

"Of course he's got a last name, Phil." She giggles.

"Well . . ."

"I don't know what it is. But I'm sure it wouldn't mean anything to you. When I told him I knew you, he said he didn't know who you were."

"How long has he been on the fire department?"

"I don't know. But I heard him telling another guy he had six years to go, whatever that means."

It means he's been on fourteen years. You can retire with a full pension after twenty. And he'd have to have been living under a fire truck not to have heard of me.

"Kadie, did you tell Ellyn about running into me?"

"Yeah, that's why we were talking about you."

"And did you tell her I was taking my cat into the vet and leaving him there for the weekend?"

"I think so. Why?"

"I was just wondering."

"No, you weren't. Come on, Phil, there's more to it than that. What's going on?"

That's a question I don't want to answer. Even if I don't, there's a chance that Kadie will call Ellyn and start asking questions. Fortunately, another call-waiting signal is beckoning.

198

"Kadie, I've got another call. I better take it. I'll call you back and explain it all later."

"Okay, well—"

"Good luck with your realtor."

"Thanks, I—"

I click her off and click on the other line. A male voice asks if I can hold for Burt Levison.

"No, I can't." Click. That should leave them scratching their heads at bit.

Not for long. The phone starts ringing the instant I hang it up.

I look at Frankie. "Don't answer it, it's Burt."

We both stand there staring at the phone until the message machine goes on in Frankie's office.

"Well, that sounded interesting," Frankie says. "So your ex-girlfriend wants to move into our neighborhood?"

"No, that won't happen. But I did learn something interesting."

"What's that?"

"I think the man with my cat is a woman."

Twenty-nine

Her name is Ellyn Miller," I tell Frankie, as I page through the phone book.

She nods. "The one whose cat you killed." She raises her hand. "Excuse me. Whose cat died while in your care."

"Thank you. She lives near Purr & Bark. And the interesting part is she has a boyfriend named Zack who's a fireman."

"Zachary Taylor?"

"Kadie doesn't know his last name. But he's been on the fire department a long time, and he told her he's never heard of me."

"Hmm. I wonder where he's been hiding."

"Maybe with her at . . . here it is: 5313 West Wilson." I write down the phone number on a sheet from one of my WYWFO pads.

"I think we should go over there and confront her rather than call," Frankie says.

"I agree. And I want to be sure it's her before we do. You don't know how embarrassed I felt going to Ron Ostrow's house last week."

"Maybe you'll have to call him up and apologize."

"It wasn't that embarrassing."

I call Pat and get four cats. I leave them a message that we've come up with new information about the current whereabouts of Phull and the whereabouts of Abby Nelson on the night her husband was killed. I give him the cellphone number in case we're not home when he gets back.

Frankie wants to know who I'm calling next.

"Scratch & Sniff. I want to find out if Ellyn is a customer there."

"Good idea."

But it doesn't amount to much. I get another recording, this one advising that the vet's office is closed until further notice. Abby Nelson is the person making the announcement, and I can tell from a murmured meow that Bobo is right in sync with her on that. I think about leaving a message, but I don't want to prompt a return call from Abby, and I'm not sure Madge will be the one monitoring the machine.

I hang it up. "Pat said Madge would be working there all day," I say.

"Maybe she's out getting her bunions worked over."

"Or maybe she's just not answering. Would you like to take a ride over there?"

"Sure. It beats sitting home here hiding out from our lawyer."

We drive to the vet's office with the windows rolled down. A southerly breeze has sent the clouds packing. We haven't had a frost yet, so you can't call it Indian summer. But the city is in a bonus situation, and everybody knows it. The parks are filled with kids and moms and nannies, and the Park District work crews are down to their T-shirts. Frankie is appalled at the high number of bad tattoos. It's a great day to recover your cat. I'm feeling as if that's about to happen. I can barely wait to see the little spray can again.

Not surprisingly, the parking lot outside the vet's office has several spaces available. I park the LeBaron next to a silver Mercedes with a license plate worth noting: ABBY. Evidently, Dr. Nelson's wife has risen far enough out of her funk to come in and lift a hand. I glance in the rear window and see something else notable—an infant's car seat. That in itself is not a surprising sight, even if Abby Nelson does not have children. It's the customization that grabs my attention.

There's no telling just how many modifications have been made, but they clearly were done with great care and thought. The overall result is inventive and comical. The seat itself is a super plush perch, more throne than chair, made of velour or possibly velvet, in a deep rich shade of gold. The arms are soft and furry, padded with a spiraling wrap of scarves, made of cashmere or possibly alpaca, maybe a blend of the two.

"Well," I say, "Bobo sure gets to ride in style."

"I don't see any lap belt. Maybe she belts him in with her brassiere."

I feel the need for a belt of coffee so we stop in White Hen before going to the vet's office. When I see Edith, I almost reconsider, but she's busy helping a guy organize lunch meats behind the sorry excuse for a deli counter. While searching for a lid that fits my cup, I take in part of their conversation.

"So, Edith, I hear today's your last day," he says.

"That's right."

"What're you going to do for money?"

"Don't worry about me, Henry. I've got enough."

"What did you do—win the lotto?"

"Don't I wish."

A hand-printed sign on the door to Purr & Bark indicates that the office is closed. Voices from behind it indicate that there are at least two people inside. Their tone suggests that it's two women. Their laughter suggests that neither of them is deep in mourning.

"Sounds like the Wide-Load Widow and the Silver Slipper are having a party," Frankie says.

"The slippers are pink."

202

"But that wouldn't be alliterative."

"According to Pat, Madge hates Abby's guts."

"Maybe tragedy has brought them closer together."

I try the doorknob. It's locked. I try it again just in case it's sticking. It's not.

I knock, three times, hard.

That stops the laughter and the voices, but it doesn't get a response.

I knock again. No response. Again. No response. The fourth time is something of a charm.

Madge's voice snaps at us from close range. Evidently she has moved right to the door. "The office is closed."

"Madge, it's Phillip Moony."

That proves to be a real conversation stopper. After about five seconds, I add some detail. "Commander Ryan's friend."

That also takes a few seconds to register.

"I'm sorry, Mr. Moony, we're closed."

"I just need to talk to you for a moment."

She takes a few moments to think that one over. "I'm sorry, Mr. Moony, I'm not supposed to let anybody in."

The pauses between responses suggest that Madge is either thinking very slowly or conferring with her companion. My bet is that Abby Nelson is pulling the strings, and I'd be willing to put a lot of money on it.

I look at Frankie. "I don't think they want us to know that Abby is in there."

"Let's not let them know we do."

I talk back to the door. "You don't need to let me in, Madge. I just need to get some information about one of the customers."

"I told Mr. Ryan everything I know, Mr. Moony."

"But there's something else I need to know."

"I'm sorry, I can't give you any more information."

"Madge, someone stole my cat. All I'm trying to do is get him back. Is a woman named Ellyn Miller a customer of yours?"

"I don't know. I don't think so."

"Would you please take a moment and check the files? It's very important."

"I'm sorry, Mr. Moony, I can't."

Well, we're not leaving until you do." I knew Frankie wouldn't be able to stand by silently for too long.

"Who's that?"

"I'm his wife. The one who told you we wanted our cat neutered but you somehow managed to forget."

"That wasn't my fault."

"Whose fault was it?"

"You'll have to ask Mr. Ryan."

"What does he have to do with it?" Frankie and I ask the same question at the same time. Thanks to the convenience of cellular technology, I get the opportunity to ask the same question of Pat at that same moment.

But I don't. I want to ask that one in person. I simply tell him where we are and that we're having a difficult time with Madge. He says he'll be right over, as soon as he feeds the cats.

"Are you saying Mr. Ryan kidnapped our cat?" Frankie's voice is raised in disbelief, with some indignation thrown in.

"Heavens no. He wouldn't do a thing like that. He just told me not to let Dr. Nelson neuter him. He said you wouldn't mind, that you'd understand." Madge's answers are coming rapid-fire now. She's either too upset to take her barking orders from Abby, or the widow and Bobo have fled the room.

"Ellyn Miller, Madge," I say. "Would you please check the files?"

"I'm looking, I'm looking." Her voice is farther away. When she speaks again, she's back at the door.

"Oh, yes, here it is. Ellyn Miller. She has three cats. Alvin, Simon and . . . Oh, no, two cats. Oh dear."

"What's the matter?"

"This is the lady whose cat died last year. Theodore. Her

boyfriend is the one who was calling Dr. Nelson and threatening to kill him."

I look at Frankie, who breaks briefly into song. "And Bingo was his name-o."

"Thank you very much, Madge. You've been very helpful."

"So, is that all?"

"Yes." I pause to let her have her sigh of relief. "No, one more thing."

Another sigh comes, and if it can be heard through the door, you know it has to be one of impatience. "What is it?"

"You can tell Mrs. Nelson there that it was a real dumb idea to put that syringe in my trash can."

"Mrs. Nelson isn't here."

"Sure she is."

"No, she's not! And I don't know anything about any syringe!"

Only one of these claims appears to be true.

The truthful one is confirmed by a sudden shriek from around the corner of the building. The falsehood is revealed on my way to investigate the shriek. As I pass a green Ford Escort parked next to Abby Nelson's Mercedes, I notice a ratty, stained trench coat on the front passenger seat. The window is open only a crack, but the odor of cat business that my neighbor Melvin reported is still overwhelming. I don't stop to let it overwhelm me. With Abby Nelson letting loose another scream, I simply file it away that she was not the bag lady Melvin saw in the alley.

Abby's shrieks aren't loud enough to curdle my blood, but if I had a beer in my hand, they'd probably do some interesting damage to that. They're certainly loud enough to bring Edith out of White Hen to see what's going on. She gets to the lot right about the time one of the screams is followed by the screech of brakes.

I can tell the screams are from Abby, because they're partly intelligible, at least to me. But I have the advantage of knowing the name of her cat. Someone who doesn't might simply hear "No! no! no! no!" But a better-trained ear can detect some B's in there.

I reach the sidewalk in just a few seconds, but it takes longer than that to locate Abby Nelson in my sights. She's partially blocked from view by the wheels of the mail truck stopped in the middle of the street, and my eyes just naturally start their search for her at eye level, not street level. By the time I see her, she's no longer doing any screaming. The fact is, she's not even moving.

It's been a few years since I've had to reconstruct an accident scene, but I haven't lost my touch. Besides, this one is a cinch. It takes all of about three seconds.

Abby came out the back door of the building into the alley, presumably to get away from Frankie and me. She may have been planning to hide there, or perhaps she didn't put it together right away that we were standing out near her car and she wouldn't be able to sneak off. When she and Bobo got to the street, he spotted something that made him abandon his perch. Possibly it was a bird or a squirrel across the street in Jefferson Park, but I suspect it was the pair of miniature poodles with pink bows that are now watching the scene unfold from the north side of Lawrence Avenue. When her beloved cat darted into the street, Abby Nelson decided to chase after him. But Abby is not nearly as nimble as Bobo, and the reflexes of the postal worker piloting the mail truck are not nearly as quick. Judging by the length of the skid marks, they're not quick at all. Either that, or he was going way too fast.

The driver stumbles as he climbs out of the truck. He's small, white, thin-to-bald in the hair department, sixty years old at least. He stares down at the prone, twisted body of Abby, oblivious to the crowd that is gathering rapidly—basketball players from the park, postal patrons, dog walkers and stroller pushers. In a few minutes, they'll be joined by curious motorists, postal workers from the loading docks and cops from the station house two blocks away. I feel certain that Edith is already back inside White Hen calling them.

"Crazy fucking broad!"

He's got that one right, but I don't like the way he says it. I expect to hear a whole lot more concern from drivers of vehicles that hit pedestrians, even when it's not their fault.

I move right past him and go to the mangled body that's wedged under the left front wheel of his truck. He follows and catches up with me just as I start to kneel down. At close range, I get a very strong hint of what the guy had for lunch. You can be sure it wasn't tea with Millicent Melrose.

"I swear, I never even saw the crazy bitch!" Why he feels compelled to tell his tale to me, I don't know. I just know that at the present moment, I'm not interested in hearing it.

I shove him away from me, and he tips over. "If you didn't see her, then why the hell did you stop?"

He gets to his feet and points down at me. "Hey, it's a federal offense to assault a postal worker!" His tone is closer to whining than yelling.

"And I think there's a local ordinance about truck drivers drinking their goddamn lunch!"

That seems to sober him up a little. Enough that I can turn my attention to Abby Nelson. Enough to make him think about working on his alibi.

"I haven't been drinking!" This time he's addressing the whole assembled throng. "The crazy broad ran right out in front of me."

I wave him away without looking up. "Oh, shut up and save it for the cops." The sound of approaching sirens indicates he won't have long to wait.

I suppose I'm giving the guy so much trouble because I know there's so little I can do for Abby Nelson. I have to work hard at controlling my urge to retch, which means I'm out of shape at what I used to do for a living. It also means that she is a real fright for the eyes.

It's too warm a day for a fur coat, but I guess Abby didn't

hear the weather report. Or maybe she had some sixth sense that she was going to be very cold sometime today. But the kind of cold she's experiencing you just don't warm up from.

It's not the blood that makes her look so horrifying, though there's enough of that to make the squeamish squirm. The really chilling visual effect is somewhat obscured by the bulky fur wrapped around her torso. Because of that, it takes even me a moment to realize that from the shoulders down, Abby Nelson is lying on her back. Which, trust me, is not the position you want to be in when your face is kissing the ground.

"Oh, Jesus." The voice of my wife comes as a comfort to me. As I look up, I see that she is being comforted by Pat Ryan.

"Broken neck?" he says, offering a question for which he doesn't need an answer.

I nod and look down to see Bobo pressing his nose into Abby Nelson's blood-streaked blond hair.

"There's nothing you can do at all?" Frankie says, another question that requires no answer.

"I'm afraid old Bobo's doing all that can be done."

I bend down and stroke the big furry cat. He purrs, but I can tell his heart's not in it. He meows, pulls away from me and sizes up Frankie a moment before staking out the turf between Pat's legs. I guess he can sense someone who's a soft touch for cats. But there's no way Pat will be able to duplicate the seating arrangement to which he's become accustomed.

"Moony, you again already? This is only my first run of the shift."

I don't need to look to identify the voice of Van McNulty. But I do and I shrug before pulling Abby Nelson's fur up to cover her head.

"And I'm oh for two saving Nelsons this week."

Thirty

We retreat to the parking lot to let the folks in blue do their job. I'm also hoping to melt into the crowd, in case a certain drunken postal worker manages to convince one of them to question me.

"Well," Pat says, "you'll be glad to know we've been cleared in Nelson's murder."

"How did that come about?"

"Dan Hynes is a smart guy. He's also very reasonable. He was pissed about the newspaper item, but once he calmed down and I laid it all out for him, he got it. He's not a Dick Slopitch fan to start with. Plus the DNA report came back from the lab. The skin shavings left on Nelson's arms belonged to a female."

"That clears you," I say. "But I'm supposed to be the needle guy."

"Don't worry about it. I told you: Hynes is a reasonable guy. Plus I found out he's a friend of Joe Carney's. He's as guilt-ridden as I was about not going to see him. We're going up there next week together, to play a little poker. You want to be the fourth?"

Frankie shoots me a cautioning glance. "Never eat at a

place called Pops, never play poker with three retired cops."

"Yeah, yeah, Nelson Algren," Pat says. "And never sleep with a woman whose problems are bigger than your own. That's why I never got married."

A woman whose problems appear to be much bigger than Pat's approaches from the street. "Oh, Mr. Ryan, isn't it just terrible?"

Pat puts his arm around Madge's shoulder and looks downright awkward doing it. I have a feeling that's only partly due to the presence of Bobo on his other arm.

"Oh, Bobo, there you are, I've been looking all over for you." She looks at Pat. "Here, I can take him, Mr. Ryan. Isn't it all just terrible?"

Pat surrenders the cat. "I don't know, Madge. I had the impression you weren't all that fond of Mrs. Nelson."

"Oh, well, I wasn't." Madge backs away. "But I didn't want anything terrible like this to happen to her."

Pat nods. "Of course not. By the way, have you ever met my friend Phil Moony? And his wife, Frankie Martin?" He looks at us. "This is Madge Kelly."

"Oh, yes, I've met them both. They're the people whose cat was taken. I was just giving them some information when the accident happened." She looks at me. "I'm sorry if I seemed difficult, but Mrs. Nelson was insisting I shouldn't tell you anything."

"I see. And then she left."

"Yes."

"And now she's gone."

"Yes, it's so shocking."

"Having a dead person around can be awfully convenient when you need to deflect blame." Frankie's observation is directed to me, but deflects off Madge.

"I beg your pardon." Madge does a pretty good job of looking bewildered, before changing the subject. "So you think Ellyn Miller is the one who has your cat?"

I nod. "Yeah, I'm pretty sure." In answer to Pat's glance,

I explain, "A girlfriend of an ex-girlfriend. She's dating Zachary Taylor."

"And, Mr. Ryan, he's also the one who threatened Dr. Nelson that time. Do you think they're the people who killed him?"

"No, Madge, I don't." Pat offers her a trace of a smile while shaking his head.

"Oh, really?" Madge does only a passable job of covering her disappointment. "Well, I better take Bobo inside." She turns to us. "I do hope you find your cat. And if you have any more questions—"

"Yes, just one," I say.

"Of course, what is it?"

A voice from behind us distracts me from asking my question. "That's the guy! Over there, in the yellow windbreaker."

Without turning around, I realize that I've just been fingered by the driver of the mail truck. I also realize that I'm wearing my favorite jacket, a gift from my wife. It was a goody-bag item from a golf junket hosted by my ex-congressman Dan Rostenkowski, before he left Washington for a country club slammer in Wisconsin. Frankie said she found it in Lincoln Park, and I've never been sure whether she meant at a resale shop or on a bench near the driving range. Right now, I'm sure that it's soaked through with sweat. Abby Nelson wasn't the only one who didn't hear the weather report.

When I turn to face the music, I'm pleasantly surprised. The cop who's coming over to talk to me is smiling. Her smile seems directed at me at first, but as she gets closer, I can see that it's meant for the guy next to me.

She gives him a nod. "Commander Ryan, I talked to Dad. He was thrilled. Thank you."

"Don't mention it. And I'm going back."

"That's what I hear. And now I'm afraid I have to ask Mr. Moony a question."

"I understand."

As soon as Audrey Carney looks at me, the smile starts to leave her face. "Mr. Moony, the driver of the truck says that you assaulted him."

"Officer Carney, that's not—"

"He didn't assault anyone!" A bystander has decided to act as my guardian angel. I hear they're taking on all sorts of forms these days, but I'll bet this is the first one on record wearing a Budweiser T-shirt and dirty jeans separated by a band of hairy flesh. "This guy didn't assault nobody, officer. He was trying to save the lady's life. And the mailman, he went over and pushed him while he was kneeling down. This guy just gave him a little shove to get out of the way so he could help the lady. And then the mailman, he starts screaming bloody murder about federal offenses."

Carney holds up her hand in a stop sign. My angel goes right through it.

"It's the damn unions, that's the problem. They think they can get away with anything."

"All right! Enough!" Carney hasn't yet perfected that tone of finality that only cops can pull off. But it works on my guy.

She looks at me. "Is that what happened, Mr. Moony?"

I'm not all that comfortable being saved by an anti-Labor voice, but I'm also not about to quibble with details. I nod. "Yeah, that's it."

The good news is that she decides to give me a pass. The bad news is that I've got a new friend. He wants me to know this is the first real time he's ever seen a head completely turned around like that; the only other time was in that movie, what was it called, *The Exorcist*. He wants to buy me a drink, he knows a place right around the corner; he's on his way back from there right now, as a matter of fact, believe it or not.

At times like this, it's good to have your real guardian angel around. Pat nudges the guy with his elbow and flashes his gold star. With Madge looking on admiringly, he demonstrates the mastery of tone that Officer Carney should be aiming for. "Buddy, get lost."

I thought Madge would have taken the opportunity to get lost herself, but she's hanging in there with Bobo still hanging on her. "You said you had another question for me, Mr. Moony."

"Yes, I do." It almost seems like a low blow right now, except that I've still got a fresh memory of sweating out the car ride with the syringe last night. "Madge, when you and Mrs. Nelson murdered Dr. Nelson, did you hold his arms or put in the needle?"

As I ask the question, it occurs to me that I might cause Madge to let go of Bobo and cause another car accident. But she tightens her grip and digs in her heels.

"What? I have no idea what you're talking about, and I resent your accusation." She looks at Pat. "Mr. Ryan?"

He shrugs with his eyes. "Phil, maybe this isn't the right time." I think Madge was hoping for a lot more support than that.

"Pat, the trench coat that the lady with the syringe was wearing last night is on the seat of her car."

"What? What car?" Madge is shouting now, and some of the street watchers are turning back to look at us.

"The green Ford Escort." I nod left with my head toward the car parked two spaces away.

"That's not my car! I don't even own a car!"

"Then whose is it?"

"How the hell should I know?" Madge's snap has grown into a snarl, and I'm starting to think I shouldn't blame her.

Another bystander joins the conversation. A short chunky guy wearing a White Sox T-shirt and a White Hen Pantry apron. It's Henry, Edith's partner in lunch meats.

"What, you mean the Escort? That's Edith's." He looks over his shoulder. "Hey, Edith, isn't that your car? The Escort?"

As I turn, I see the White Hen clerk standing on the driver's side of the car in question.

"Yes. Why?" Edith gets the answer to her question when she sees my face. It's clear that she doesn't like either.

"I didn't do anything," she says. But her movements say otherwise.

She pulls away from the gray-haired woman she's talking to and yanks open the car door. As she starts to get in, she glances around the crowded lot and realizes the futility of trying to make a getaway. You could get out of a Bulls game lot faster than this one right now. It's one of the reasons I prefer on-street parking.

Edith remains standing by the open door as we approach.

"You weren't wearing that coat in the alley behind my house last night?" I ask.

"No," I wasn't.

"A neighbor of mine can identify you."

"It wasn't me."

"Slip a handful of Valiums into Dr. Nelson's tea, maybe? You used to be a nurse, right? That was a real good job you did with the needle."

"No!"

"That's why you were so insistent on bringing over his tea," Madge says. "He said it tasted funny. But you forgot my Slushie. She looks bewildered, then crestfallen, as another revelation dawns on her. "Mr. Ryan, you thought I killed Dr. Nelson? How on earth could you think such a thing?"

She doesn't give him time to answer. Which is okay, because I'm sure he doesn't have one ready. As she takes off running toward the door of the vet's office, I hear her start to sob. But it's the sound of her slippers slapping on the sidewalk that makes me feel sad.

"Madge! Wait!" The magic isn't in Pat's tone this time. That's because he's pleading instead of commanding.

He starts after her, stops, glances at Edith, then at us. "I think we owe that lady a big apology."

Frankie nods. "Boy, do we ever."

Pat growls at White Hen Henry. "Were you working Monday night?"

"Monday, let's see, I think—"

"Monday. The night Dr. Nelson was killed!"

"Oh, yeah, that Monday; sure I was."

"Do you remember what time Edith went on her break?"

"Sure, six o'clock, just like she—"

"Shut up, Henry!" Edith yelps over the roof of her car. "Would you shut the hell up?"

"That would be good advice for you too, Edith," Pat says. "Be sure to get yourself a good lawyer."

Edith isn't taking any advice right now, no matter how good, not even her own. I think that's because she's being provoked by someone who's not as sympathetic as Pat.

"How much did Abby pay you, Edith," I ask. "It wasn't the lotto, but how much?"

"It wasn't about the money, you fool," she shouts. "It was about the cats. He was going to kill *all* of Abby's cats. All of them! And he calls himself an animal lover. He got exactly what he deserved."

"Time to button your lip, Edith" Pat says. He turns to the street and bellows for Officer Carney.

She arrives in short order and a little short of breath. "Commander Ryan, is there a problem?"

"Audrey, we have very strong reason to believe that this woman over here was involved in the killing of Dr. Nelson."

A look of recognition spreads over Carney's face as she sizes up Edith. "You're the one who brought us the coffee the other night."

"Yes, that's right." There's a faint sound of hope in Edith's voice. "You remember."

"Yeah, I do." Audrey Carney's nose crinkles as her memory evokes a wince. "It tasted funny."

215

"You're lucky you didn't get the batch she brewed up for Dr. Nelson," Frankie says.

"What do you want me to do?" Carney asks Pat. "You know I can't hold her unless you've got something solid to go on."

"Oh, we've got something solid. And I don't think she's going anywhere too soon anyway."

Carney takes a look around the lot. "Yeah, I guess you're right about that."

"Do you think you could radio Detective Clay and see if she can come up here right away?"

"Sure. But I think Detective Slopitch is the primary investigator on that case."

"You've met Detective Slopitch. I think it would be nice if we gave this one to his female partner, don't you?"

She smiles. "Yes, Commander, I see what you mean."

Thirty-one

"Madge, I'm going to go off with my friends now." Pat talks to the locked door of the vet's office. "Are you sure you're going to be all right?"

He gets the same response that he did to his apology a moment earlier: "Go away."

"I can come back later if you'd like."

"*Go* away."

"I really am sorry. I want you to know that."

"Leave me alone. Would you just leave me alone?"

Pat sighs and frowns and sighs again.

Frankie gives him a tender pat on the shoulder. "This is really hard for you, isn't it, Pat?"

He shrugs. "I'll get over it, don't you worry."

I follow his gaze across Lawrence Avenue to Jefferson Park. All the action is finished now, and the neighborhood is back to its usual dull self, though brightened by the unusually warm weather. The shirts and skins are back at it on the basketball court, the nannies and moms are chattering to each other in Polish while their young ones frolic on the playlot. Anyone who happens to be passing through would have no idea what has transpired over the last hour. The mail truck has been moved to the curb, the road flares have burned to ashes, the curiosity seekers have gone back about their business, and the cops have gone back to work. Mrs. Edwin Nelson has been carried off in Van McNulty's rig, one cranky postal worker has been carted off in a squad car, and White Hen Pantry is short one counter clerk for the evening.

Edith left voluntarily a few minutes ago, following Detective Candy Clay down to the Grand Central station house for questioning. Clay let her call a lawyer before they left, and Pat says if the guy's any good, there's a chance she may never be charged.

"It all depends on the evidence. They can link the Valium to the tea and they can put her fingerprints on the cup, but they can't prove she put the Valium in it. As for the actual killing, her prints weren't on the syringe they found."

"What about the trench coat?" Frankie asks. "Do you think they could do something with that?"

"It got her down to the station, but whether they can do more with it is anybody's guess. It depends on whether they can get a warrant to search her car. Your neighbor will have to identify her as the lady poking around in your trash. And even if he does, they can't prove she left that syringe there, because they didn't find one when they searched."

"Where's that syringe now?" I ask.

"I think it will probably be found with the trench coat. The cops may never see it, but it'll sure make Edith lose some sleep."

"When did you have time to do that?"

Pat shoots me a look that could stop a train. "Do what? Did I say I did anything?" He looks at Frankie.

"Nope, I sure didn't hear you."

"Oh, well, let's get on to the really important stuff. Let's go get your cat."

With all the one-way streets in the neighborhood, we

could have walked to Ellyn Miller's house faster than it takes to drive there in the LeBaron. The block of Wilson Avenue that Ellyn lives on is all tiny yellow brick bungalows, the same construction design as the homes on Ron Ostrow's block in Edison Park. But Ellyn's little plot has a distinctive touch: a driveway.

There's a Nissan Pathfinder parked in it. It's white, and the license plate has no numbers, just letters: ZACK.

I pull to the curb across the street. "I'd say that fits Millicent's description, wouldn't you?"

Pat shrugs with his head. "She said it was a sports car."

"To an old gal like Millicent, it probably looks kind of sporty."

"I told you before, she ain't so old. Let's take a few extra minutes and be sure."

Even with the early rush-hour traffic starting to build on Milwaukee Avenue, we make it to Millicent Melrose's house in less than five minutes. Pat hops out of the car quickly and says he'll go to the door.

Millicent answers his knock from a bedroom window. "Patrick, you're early!"

Pat's face is blocked from view, but judging by the rush of red to his neck, I'm sure he looks embarrassed.

Half a minute later, Millicent appears at the front door. "What a pleasant surprise." She glances at her watch. "I wasn't expecting you for another two hours and twelve minutes."

"She's precise, I'll give her that," Frankie says.

"She used to be a librarian."

Pat's immediate response is barely audible, but I can make out something about coming back later. "We think we've located the man who stole Phil's cat," he says, speaking again at normal volume. "Now you said the man leaving Dr. Nelson's office with Phull had a white sports car . . ."

"That's right."

"Are you sure it was a sports car?"

"I'm positive. It was just like the one O. J. drove."

Pat glances over his shoulder at me.

"Close enough?" I ask.

"Yeah, I'd say so." He turns back to Millicent and lowers his voice again.

Her response comes at a much higher volume. "If you really want to be sure, shouldn't I come along to identify him?"

"Would you be willing to do that?"

"I'd be happy too. It sounds exciting. Wait a minute while I get my coat."

"It's seventy degrees; you won't need one."

Millicent is gone before Pat's fashion advice reaches her. She returns in a pink windbreaker emblazoned with the phrase READERS ARE LEADERS. She holds out her hand for Pat to help her down the steps. He's beaming as he leads her to the car.

"My, don't they look cute," Frankie says.

"Yup. Like a pair of kittens."

"Hello, Mr. Moony, how are you?" Millicent says, as she gets into the backseat.

"Call me Phil, please."

"Okay. And you must be Frankie. Patrick has told me so much about you."

"It's a pleasure. Thanks for being so willing to help."

"Oh, I don't mind at all."

We drive back to Ellyn Miller's house Long Island style, guys in the front, gals in the back. Pat seems nervous, and I don't think it has anything to do with anticipating a confrontation with Ellyn or her beau. But he's making a plan, just the same.

"Okay, now when we get there, Phil and I will go up to the house first. Millicent and Frankie, you wait in the car until I signal for you."

"What will the signal be, dear? Will you whistle for us?"

That prompts an all-out laugh from my wife, and brings the blood rushing back to Pat's face.

"He'll let out a big meow," I say.

When we get to Ellyn's block, I can see the Pathfinder still parked in her driveway. I also see a woman and man parked on either side of it. It's a perfect day to wash your car, though personally I find the drive-thru more romantic.

This time I pull up to the curb on Ellyn's side of the street. As I open the door she looks our way, brushing away strands of hair with the back of a hand that's holding a soapy sponge.

"Oh, shit, it's Moony!"

"What?" Ellyn's washing partner stops and looks at me through the windows of the Pathfinder.

I have to stop and rub my eyes in disbelief. I'm assuming this is Zack, but the guy bears an uncanny resemblance to Ron Ostrow.

"It's Moony, Zack, he's here!"

I move toward his side of the car to get a look at the guy that's not tempered through glass.

He moves along the side of the car to get a better look at me. "Don't worry, Ellyn, I'll handle it."

My view is clear when he gets to the back bumper and I reach the driveway. We're about ten yards apart, which is about all of Ellyn's yard. He's holding a garden hose in his hand.

Damn if the guy doesn't look exactly like Ron Ostrow. Damn if the guy isn't Ron Ostrow!

"Holy shit," I say.

"What's that?" Pat asks me.

The answer comes from behind us, a shout out of the mouth of my wonderful wife, who has ignored Pat's admonition and gotten out of the car with Millicent.

"Ostrow! What the hell are you doing here?"

"That's him," Millicent says. "That's the man with your cat; I'm positive."

"Ostrow? Who's Ostrow? Zack?" Ellyn looks confused, but then don't we all.

All except Ostrow, who looks as if he swallowed a turd and stammers like it's still caught in his throat. "Uh, Ellyn, go inside and get his cat."

"I don't get it," Pat says. "Is this . . . ?"

I nod. "My old partner."

"And Zachary Taylor?"

I nod again. "One and the same."

"Oh, I get it, now I get it." Pat starts to laugh.

"Get what? What's so funny?" Ellyn looks at Ostrow. "Zack?"

He wheels and snaps. "Ellyn, don't ask any questions. Just go in the house, go down to the basement, and get the damn cat."

Ellyn follows his orders, but very slowly, backing toward the front steps.

I nod and smile. "Hello, Ellyn, how've you been?"

"Oh, shut up." She turns and starts up the steps.

Frankie moves up beside me and begins giving Ron the eye. "Ostrow, you creep, I don't believe it."

While raising his hands to shrug, Ron accidentally sprays himself, but seems barely to notice.

"Phil, it all started as a joke, man. This old girlfriend of yours came to this party we were having, and she and Ellyn were talking about how you were watching her cat that time and it died. I knew you were leaving your cat for the weekend on account of seeing your wife there. It was Ellyn's idea. She has a hard-on for that vet, on account of one of her new cats died there last year. It seemed perfect, you know?"

"Yeah, I get it," I say. "Kill two birds with one cat."

"Exactly. We were planning on returning him to you."

"Yeah? Like when?" Frankie asks.

"Soon. Tonight or tomorrow."

Frankie scoffs. "Sure you were."

"I'm serious, we weren't going to keep him. I mean it, it was all just a joke."

"You took a lot of risk for a joke, Ron," I say. "Weren't you worried about being recognized? They know you at Nelson's office."

"No, that was the beauty of it. I heard the regular lady say she wasn't going to be in Monday morning."

"Yeah, beautiful," Pat says. "A perfect plan." He looks at me. "Phil, you had to do emergency medicine with this jag-off? My condolences."

"Listen, I'm sorry, it was a dumb thing to do. I did it for Ellyn."

Frankie snorts. "What a thoughtful guy you are."

"Yeah, I know, it was dumb." Ostrow glances over his shoulder at the front door, then back at us. "Uh, listen, guys. Please don't say anything more to Ellyn about . . . well, you know. I'll do anything for you, I swear."

"Like what?" Frankie says. "Wash our car?"

"Sure, anything, I mean it."

"Yuck!" Ellyn is coming out the door. "Your damn cat just sprayed me, Moony."

"Serves you right," Frankie says. She crouches down with hands out, encouraging Phull to run to her. But he has another destination in mind. Like Bobo, Phull can pick a real cat fancier out of a crowd.

Pat picks him up and starts stroking his head. Millicent moves over and stands beside him. "Oh, Patrick, he's adorable."

"Yuck, I hate that dumb cat." Ellyn starts in wiping her shirt with the car sponge.

"Gosh, Ellyn, unlucky with cats, unlucky with men. And still your same cheerful old self, huh?"

"Oh, shut up, Phil."

"I really feel sorry for Ron here when you finally figure out the game he's been playing with you."

"What? Who's Ron?"

"Come on, Phil, please, I'm begging you."

"Gosh, Ellyn. You mean you haven't met the family yet?"

"What? What family? Zack? What's he talking about?"

Ostrow avoids her glance and looks at me. "Fuck you, Moony."

"How have you been getting away with it, Ron? You didn't tell Robin that you went from forty-eight to seventy-two off? What do you do when she thinks you've got a Daley Day?"

"Robin? Who's Robin? Zack—talk to me!"

Right now, old Ron has words only for me. Ostrow drops the hose, spreads his legs and assumes a fighting position. "Okay, c'mon, let's go, jagoff. This time, I'll kick your ass."

This time, he very well might. Dave Zezel said Ron's been lifting weights and he looks it. The only thing I've been lifting on a regular basis is pints of Leinenkugels at a German bar on Irving Park Road.

Instead of clenching his fists, Ron keeps his hands open. I wonder if he's added any of the martial arts to his résumé.

This gives me pause, but it's not what's stopping me from answering the bell. After all, I've got Pat Ryan for backup. The thing that's stopping me is the memory of the first time Ostrow and I tangled and how lousy I felt afterward. Hell, I felt lousy while it was going on. Besides, one phone call to his wife, and I can do a whole lot more damage than a kick in the nuts.

Of course, I don't have a chance to confer with my wife on this point. I think I mentioned that she's kind of old-fashioned.

She's also more direct. Plus she's got great aim, and a very pointy pair of alligator boots, which she bought in Milan.

And great timing. She delivers it right as he starts forward, soccer style, with just the proper angle of ascent. Ostrow doesn't know what hit him at first, but he knows where he's been hit right away.

So much for the fighting stance. The knees go first, then the hands. They're clenched now, no time for kung fu. Ron should have taken a class in shiatsu massage. You can be damn sure he's not going to get one from Ellyn.

"Ron, stay right where you are," I say. "Try to get up, and Frankie's going to show you a move she learned from her uncle, back in Sicily."

Ostrow's mouth forms to make a reply, but no words come out. Just one pathetic groan.

I look at Ellyn. "You're a nurse. What do you recommend for him—ice?"

Icy silence is the response I get. As we turn away, I can feel a chilly gust from the northwest. The sun is setting in the land beyond O'Hare. Indian summer is over.

"Perhaps the cat has gotten her tongue," Millicent says.

She giggles, and Pat laughs harder than he should. Ellyn runs sobbing into her little yellow bungalow. It looks like a place you could have a real good cry in. In the three days that Phull's been there, he could have tagged every wall.

Just before we reach the car, Ostrow recovers his power of speech. "Moony, don't tell Robin! Please, don't tell Robin."

"You can relax a bit, Ron. I'll probably flip a coin."

Thirty-two

Frankie is the first to speak when we get in the car. "Boy, did that ever feel good," she says, rubbing one of her boots. She's changed seating arrangements by sliding in beside me, leaving Pat wedged in the back seat next to Millicent. With Phull, they make a coosome threesome.

"How could you tell?" I ask. "With those beauties on, I'll bet you didn't feel a thing."

"I love these boots, darling. I may never take them off again."

"You will when your feet start to hurt, young lady, believe me."

There's no challenging Millicent's voice of experience, but when we talk later, I know Frankie will say she seems a wee bit literal. Right now, she's literally giving Pat a working over.

"Patrick, did you tell them yet?"

"No, Millicent, I haven't had a chance."

"Well, you've got one now, go ahead."

For a fleeting moment, I wonder if Pat's about to announce their wedding engagement. But I realize that for an old-fashioned guy like him, there'd have to be a courtship.

"Guys, I have a confession to make," Pat says.

"Yeah, we already know," I say.

"Your accomplice rolled over on you," Frankie adds.

"Who—Madge?"

"She gave you up for a Slushie."

"Jeez, I can't believe she did that."

"Patrick, that's not the point. You did something inappropriate with their pet."

"Yeah, you're right." He speaks to us. "I'm sorry, it was the wrong thing for me to do. How you want to care for your pet is your own personal decision. I should respect that." He speaks to Millicent. "How was that? Was that good?"

"Yes, very good."

He raises his voice. "But you, Moony, you lied to me, you rotten son of a bitch. You said you didn't ask to have the little guy neutered."

"You forced us into it," Frankie says. I think it's nice that she sees herself as a full partner in my crime. "You acted as an agent provocateur."

"Yeah, I suppose you're right. Well, it won't happen again, I promise."

Frankie reaches into the backseat and strokes the furry bundle on Pat's lap. "And I promise you, Phull, that we won't consider putting you under the knife ever again."

As I gaze at Pat and Phull in the rearview mirror, I begin entertaining a notion that will enable my wife to keep her vow. Considering Millicent's embrace of the multiple-cat life, Frankie won't have any objections. I pop the question when we pull up behind Pat's car.

"Pat, would you like another cat?"

"Would I, would I?"

"Harelip, harelip."

Pat starts to laugh and Frankie wants to know what's so funny.

I pat her leg with my hand. "I guess you don't know the joke about the guy with the wooden eyeball and the waitress with the harelip."

"No, and I don't think I want to."

"It's probably a guy thing," Millicent says.

Pat invites us to join them for dinner, which is just the kind of thing a guy would do on his first date. Frankie answers promptly in the negative, leaving no time for this guy to botch things up. After the good-bye hugs and purrs are finished, she answers just as promptly in the affirmative when I suggest a dinner date for the two of us.

Two blocks from the vet's office where all the confusion started, I'm pulled over by one of Chicago's finest. He's about Pat's age and forty pounds to the good, which means he's probably put in about forty years of distinguished service.

He demands my license and insurance card and asks if I know why he stopped me.

"I imagine it's because of my taillight being out, Officer. My wife just noticed that when I was backing out of our garage."

"No, that's not it. But you better get that fixed. The reason I stopped you is you don't have a city sticker."

"Damn." I slap my hand to my forehead as hard as I can. "I've got one, Officer, I just keep forgetting to put it on my windshield. My wife keeps reminding me, but . . ." I look at Frankie. "You were right, honey, I'm sorry."

As he makes the trek back to his car, she shakes her head sadly. "Oh, good one, Phil. You've really managed to elicit his sympathy." She reaches in her purse and pulls out a ten.

"I was thinking a twenty."

"Are you crazy?"

The traffic cop returns to my window holding a bundle of papers. "So, Mr. Moony, how do you want to handle this?"